"Jack? Is that you?" Abby called into the pale darkness before dawn.

"Abby? I didn't mean to wake you," he answered, standing before her barefoot, bare-chested, wearing only his jeans. "Beautiful out, isn't it?"

She sank down on the trailer step and wrapped her arms around her knees. "Just look at that sky, and that moon—and just listen to those frogs. Brr-up, Brr-up," she called softly toward the lake.

Jack dropped down beside her. "So, do you often sit in the dark making funny noises?" he asked softly, teasingly, tracing the outline of her cheek with his strong fingers.

"Never," she answered, catching his hand between her cheek and her bare shoulder. Her eyes shone like stars. "No one's ever tempted me out into the night before."

"Oh, you do know the right thing to say," he whispered, kissing the curve of her neck.

"Never have before," she repeated softly. She ran her fingers through his dark, thick hair and turned his face up to hers.

Their mouths met and clung. She suddenly felt lighter than air. She was floating, flying. "I must be dreaming," she said against his lips, but he nipped the words away with his teeth.

"No," he said. "Before, you were dreaming. This is real. . . ."

WHAT ARE *LOVESWEPT* ROMANCES?

They are stories of true romance and touching emotion. We believe those two very important ingredients are constants in our highly sensual and very believable stories in the *LOVESWEPT* line. Our goal is to give you, the reader, stories of consistently high quality that may sometimes make you laugh, sometimes make you cry, but are always fresh and creative and contain many delightful surprises within their pages.

Most romance fans read an enormous number of books. Those they truly love, they keep. Others may be traded with friends and soon forgotten. We hope that each *LOVESWEPT* romance will be a treasure—a "keeper." We will always try to publish

LOVE STORIES YOU'LL NEVER FORGET
BY AUTHORS YOU'LL ALWAYS REMEMBER

The Editors

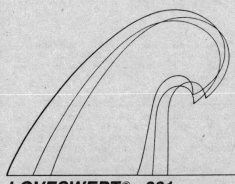

LOVESWEPT® • 281

Adrienne Staff
Paradise Café

 BANTAM BOOKS
TORONTO • NEW YORK • LONDON • SYDNEY • AUCKLAND

PARADISE CAFÉ

A Bantam Book / September 1988

For Bruce, Erica, Chris,
Mil and Mort,
Michele, Glenn, Erin and Ryan,
Lil and Sam
. . . and Patty too

with all my love!

One

"Let go of the raft!"

The words shouted from behind were lost in the roar of the water over her, the thunder of the water crashing against the sheer canyon walls and hurtling her downstream.

"Let go of the raft!" The second time she *heard* the shout, but her fingers clutched the edge of the heavy rubber raft more tightly, as tightly as she ever had held to anything in her life. Her life! Oh, Lord, she was going to die! She knew it. In the seconds after she was swept through the first rapids, her thoughts were fragmented: Death. Fear. Loss. Panic. She hadn't said good-bye to her parents. She'd never see home again. She was going to die in this ice-cold water, all alone in the rushing river, the white and green foam swirling over her face.

Moving ever downstream, Abby lashed one arm across the hump of the raft and wept, her tears instantly erased by the icy splash of spray. What was she going to do? *Oh, God*, she prayed, *oh, someone, help!* She began to scream, "Help me! Oh, help me . . . oh . . ."

Like a living thing, the river gathered itself beneath her and leaped forward. "Oh, help! Someone help me!" She felt the river surge and rise, and ahead she saw the white riffles and hanging spray that signaled the start of the next rapids.

Saw them and was taken by them in the same second.

The water was lifting and churning over rocks that were only dark, looming shadows beneath the white, foaming surface. "Oh, no, not again, no more— please!" she screamed, while the raft strained at her hold, leaping and jumping over the dark, crouched rocks, wrenching at her arms, pulling her faster and faster, the water always in her eyes and mouth and nose.

And then the third shout came from behind, loud and insistent and commanding:

"Let go of the raft!"

And her mind, or the tiny section of her mind that wasn't numbed by fear and panic and cold, remembered her guide's instructions before they ever got on the river, the damned, damned river where she was about to die. Three rules if you fall in: Point your feet downstream to cushion the blows, hold on to your life jacket, and if someone yells "Let go of the raft!" then do it!

"Oh, no. She couldn't. She couldn't! It was all she had that meant safety and hope. She couldn't. She wouldn't. . . .

"Let go of the raft! *Now!*"

She released her hold, and the raft tore downstream like a demon creature bent for hell. Flying, springing, it crashed against the looming black canyon wall.

Abby swung her arms wildly, the water swirling over her face, drowning her, choking her. But instead of the wall, her feet hit the torn rubbery side of the raft, and she bounced back away from the rocks and out into the middle of the river again.

For a moment she hung there, shocked into immobility by the memory of those looming rock walls flying at her and away. She couldn't breathe, couldn't think; her eyes were wide with fear. She hung there in the deceptive, momentary calm of one of the deep, still pools between the rapids.

The water was black there, deeper than she could imagine. She tried to kick, but her feet were numb; so were her legs. The icy numbness was sliding insidiously up her body to her waist, her chest. She felt the cold hand of death gripping her.

Screaming, she flailed at the water, aiming for the canyon wall. Anything, anything was better than the water. The wall slid by, picking up speed like a phony backdrop in a grade B movie. Fast and faster now, as the river carved into the canyon walls at a sudden angle. She could see the spiked tips of the pines growing at the cliff top above her, the ribboned layers of rock exposed on the cliff walls, the white, churning water ahead. "Help!" she screamed, the water filling her mouth. Panic brought life to her legs, and she backpedaled desperately. "Save me!"

Incredibly, another raft flew into sight, with a huge, dark-haired guide at the oars. She struggled toward this one hope. She saw the man straining against the pull of the river, his arm muscles bulging, his whole body fighting the current, fighting to save her, his arms, back, neck, hips locked in battle, slowing the raft, slowing it just enough *perhaps* to let her grasp the hands reaching out to her as she splashed closer. He fought the river, shouting "Swim, dammit! Swim!" in the same hoarse, urgent voice that had commanded her to let go of the raft. *"Come on! Swim!"*

Abby tried, but her body was too cold to obey her commands, and the river was too strong. The guide shouted a curse as the river escaped the drag of his oars and the raft leaped into the rapids and was gone and she was pulled under the foaming surface.

She felt a sharp stab of pain as she hit the rounded

hump of a boulder and was flung over it. She gave up all hope and stopped breathing, stopped thinking, stopped praying. The river swept on with her as it snaked around its next turn, and then suddenly she was trapped in a tangle of tree branches leaning like a net across the water.

As Abby felt the solid wood, sheer instinct took over and she scrambled up, sending loose gravel and rock hailing into the water. She felt the dead tree slip under her weight and climbed faster, planting one foot on the broken trunk, pulling the other up alongside, scrambling up onto the rocks until she could think, stop, and take control of her body. She dug her heels into the loose rock face of the canyon wall and spread her arms wide, her fingers prying a hold into the rock.

She was out of the water. Alive. Oh, God . . .

She started to shake and couldn't stop. Her whole body was jumping with fear and shock; her teeth were chattering. There was nothing she could do. She wanted to climb farther but couldn't, wanted to edge over just a foot or two to a notch in the wall that had grass she could grab hold of, but she couldn't. She wanted to shout for help, but couldn't; her teeth were clicking and wouldn't stop even when she bit her lips hard enough to taste blood.

A rock slid from beneath her left foot, and she screamed. She turned and pressed her body against the rock wall until it dug into her back.

Suddenly she saw movement on the cliff top across the river. Wiping her face against her shoulder, she squinted through water and tears to bring the shapes into focus. Someone was there, gesturing, shouting. "Up . . . go up!" the person yelled, pointing to the top of the canyon wall forty feet above her; she shook her head in a short, nervous jerk.

She couldn't move, couldn't answer.

The person kept shouting at her, waving, yelling at her as if she were purposely not listening, not following orders. She saw it was *her* guide, the one who had lost control and let her raft flip, flinging her and the others into the river, and the others were with him: her pal Elaine and the two fellows they had met in Estes Park who had promised that a raft trip would be such fun! Oh, dear Lord, they were all there, safe, and *she* was down here, the wall crumbling into the river below her, the water just waiting, waiting to take her again.

She squeezed her eyes shut, and tears slid down her cheeks, ran into her open mouth. Everything hurt now, her legs, her stomach, her chest whenever she breathed. *Help*, she prayed silently. *Someone help me.* In all her life she had never been so afraid. It was worse than the most awful nightmare.

Then she heard a noise above. Abby gasped, then held her breath and listened. It was a voice, a man's shout, directly overhead. She tipped her head back against the rock wall and saw a rope uncoil from the edge above and to the right. And then that dark-haired rafter swung himself over and down, sending a tiny avalanche cascading harmlessly past her and into the water. She shuddered, cringing at the splash. "Hurry," she begged.

"Hold on! I'm coming to get you," he shouted, and she let her head fall back and didn't open her eyes until she felt his hand on her shoulder.

"Don't be scared," he said softly. "You're okay now."

She didn't answer, couldn't, just kept her teeth clamped down over her bottom lip and tried to stop shaking. Tears spilled from her eyes.

He touched her face, pushing the hair and leaves and dirt back from her cheek with blunt, strong fingers. "It's okay now," he repeated, looking into her wide, terrified eyes. *Poor thing*, he thought, *poor little thing*, but aloud he said, "Are you hurt? Tell me where you're hurt."

Abby was shaking too hard to answer, so he gently ran a hand across her arms, down her ribs on one side and up over the other. Then he crouched against the rock and ran his hand over both scratched and bruised legs.

She felt cold as ice, he thought, and those wide, unblinking eyes worried him. He touched her cheek. "You're all right. Nothing's broken. You had a bad time, but I'm going to take care of you; I'm going to get you out of here. I know you're scared, but it's going to be okay." He kept stroking her face and talking, ignoring her chattering teeth, her silence. "Okay, now, I want you to take hold of this rope and pull up. I'll be under you here, pushing. We'll get you right up, just one foot at a time, hand over hand—"

She shook her head wildly, panic blinding her. She could not, would not, move, knowing she would slide back into the river like a stone.

He understood. "Okay," he answered, soothing her with his voice, his hand. "Hey, it's all right. I'll help you."

A tiny, hiccuping sob broke in her throat.

He knew he had to get her out of there, and fast. She was shaking, trembling, and there was blood on her legs, on her face. Narrowing his eyes against the glare of sun on water, he scanned the river and the canyon wall; his practiced eye said there was no way out but up. Okay, then, he'd get her up there. Now.

After wrapping the rope securely around one of his wrists, he leaned close, close enough for his breath to stir her hair. "Listen to me. All you have to do is put your arms around my neck. I'll carry you up. You just hold on." He half-turned around, offering his broad back. "Come on. Climb aboard."

"I can't." She stayed rigidly unmoving, but her face was wet with fresh tears that clung to her lashes before rolling down her cheeks.

"Shhh," he said softly. "It's going to be all right. Here we go." He locked his free hand around her wrist and pulled it over his shoulder to his chest and pushed his bulk out and away from the canyon wall. She screamed, but her other hand snapped into place around his neck, and her body clung to his, her legs wrapping around his hips like a vise.

Reaching down behind, he scooted her higher on his back; she didn't weigh anything at all, even soaking wet.

"Damn," he breathed, letting himself think for a split second about how hurt she could be, about what could have happened with that damn stupid amateur as a guide. He'd like to rip his damn ears off! And with anger fueling his muscles, he pulled them both up the slippery, crumbling rock face, finding invisible hand- and footholds, climbing with the steadily mounting exhilaration that only an avid climber can know.

If she'd loosen that choke hold around his neck it would be a lot easier, he thought, struggling for breath as his heart sledgehammered against his ribs. "Ease up," he gasped out, a mistake, because the sound of his voice made her tighten the noose of her grip.

She wanted to hold on more and more tightly, glue herself to this solid, warm, living back, climb right under his skin and hide there safe and warm. He was so big, so strong, so powerful. His voice helped to drown out the roar of water in her ears. The hardness of his muscles was better than the hardness of rock. The heat of him was better than the white glare of the sun. Her whole world narrowed to the feel of him, the safety of him, the coil and release of his muscles, the smell of his sweat. "Help me, please," she begged, the only words her chattering would allow.

"You're all right," he repeated gently. "Okay. We're almost there."

"Don't let me go. Don't drop me!"

"I won't, don't worry."

"I'm scared," she whispered against his neck.

"I know. But you're all right now. Look, there's Mike, waiting to help you up."

Sure enough, another man appeared at the top of the canyon wall and reached an arm down toward the two edging up toward him. "Almost there!" he called encouragingly. "Come on . . . come on."

"I'm comin', dammit. You just get ready to give her a hand up."

"Okay, reach on up here. I'm ready for you—"

She tried, really tried. But she couldn't loosen her grip. It was like letting go of the raft all over again, and this time she just couldn't.

"Listen, trust me. Just reach one hand up and he'll have you safe on level—"

The rest of his words were choked off by her stranglehold on his neck. "I can't!"

"Damn!" He dug his toes into a crevice the size of a matchstick and shifted her weight on his back. "Okay," he said with a gasp, "at least ease off on that hold; I can't breathe, let alone climb! Hear me?"

She pushed her face against his neck. He could feel her shaking, trembling, but her voice was a little steadier, as if she had really heard him that time. "I'm sorry," she whispered, relaxing her grip ever so slightly. Instinctively, her legs tightened around his hips. He grinned despite it all; this was one hell of a situation, and just when things had begun to look boring.

Then he started up again, every muscle and sinew complaining. The rope had cut into one hand, and his blood made the rope slick. His grip slipped once, just a fraction, but enough to make him catch his breath between clenched teeth; he heard her crying softly into his hair. He struggled to within two feet of the top, where Mike could reach down, slip his hands under her arms, and lift her straight onto the grass. Then he hoisted himself up and over.

"How did you *do* that, man?" Mike asked, his voice a croak. He was grinning, pumped up with the vicarious excitement of the climb. "Hell, Gallagher, you're a damn mountain goat!"

Jack Gallagher grinned back, his chest heaving, his heart pumping hard and strong. He bent his head to catch his breath, rested his palms against his thighs, and smiled up at the other man from beneath dark brows. "It was that or swim," he said, laughing. "Now, cut the talk. How's the girl?"

She was sitting on the grass, arms wrapped around her drawn-up knees, her forehead burrowing into them.

Jack dropped down beside her, thinking he would let her cry it out while he caught his breath, but she looked up and took his breath away completely when her eyes met his.

"Thanks," she said softly, offering a shaky little smile. "Not that I know how to thank someone who just saved my life." She could barely speak, and the words escaped in tiny pops as she found and lost her voice. "Oh, Lord, I really thought I was going to die down there." Her mouth quivered, and she shook her head, looking away from the gorge and into the trees behind them. "I thought I'd never see home again, my family . . ." Tears slid out of the corners of her eyes. Quickly, she reached up and brushed them away with the back of her hand.

He caught her hand between both of his and rubbed hard, trying to bring some warmth back to her skin. "Listen, you might feel better if you went ahead and cried."

She shook her head hard, sending her wet hair flying around her pale face.

"You had a bad time down there," he said coaxingly, knowing she realized it all too well, but knowing also, as she might not, that fear like that would claw its way out one way or another. "A good cry might help."

"If I started I'd never stop." She pulled her hand away and wrapped her arms around her knees again, trying to hold herself together. Her shoulders lifted and jumped with the shakes.

Without a thought, he pulled his "river rat" T-shirt up over his head and down over hers. "Here, put your arms through this. It's not dry, but it's a lot drier than you are. And we need to get you walking, got to get your blood moving again. Can you stand up?"

"I don't know. I'm having—trouble with sitting; I'm not sure how—how good I'll be at standing."

"Here, we'll give it a shot."

With Mike on one side and him on the other, they got her to her feet. Her knees buckled, and she sagged between them, shaky as a sapling in a high wind. Jack pulled her close, wrapping an arm around her waist. Her head came just to his shoulder, and her hair and face were cold against his warm skin. "I'd carry you, but if you can walk, it's better. What do you think?"

"I think I w-want to lie down and—and close my eyes and wake up to find this . . . was all a horrible dream." Dry, ragged sobs were gathering in her throat, and her faint, determined little smile wobbled.

"Later. Come on, let's try again." Holding her against his side, he took a few steps across the sunny glade, Mike trailing them. "There, that's better."

"Yes—I think so."

"Good. Then let's get this show on the road."

Gently, he swung her back to his side and started off on a slow walk, talking softly. "Look at these pines. Did you ever see a forest this thick, untouched? Can you smell them? And that's wild blackberry, there. It'll bloom soon, and the berries are sweet as sugar when you pick them early in the morning. . . ."

The sun was now directly overhead: Noon. It warmed the top of her head, dried her hair to a mess of sandy tangles, and lay like a blanket on her narrow shoulders. Her sobs faded to an occasional harsh hiccup, and her step steadied.

"This is an old Ute hunting trail," he said, using

his voice like a sedative. "A hundred years ago they walked here, following the deer and elk."

She looked around, seeing for the first time the trees, the thick underbrush, the light filtering down like golden dust. Drawing a deep, steadying breath, she said, "It's pretty."

She knew he wanted her to talk, to relax, and she felt bound to try. "I—I'm from Florida, and we—we have pines there too. Lots of people don't know that. And there are palms, and—and live oaks, and groves. Oh, *nothing's* as pretty as an orange grove at first light. So green, and the scent of orange blossoms in the warm air—" Tears closed her throat. "I—I thought I'd *never* see any of it again."

"You will. You've got my word on it!" He slid his hand down her arm until he caught hold of her hand. "You're going to be fine."

They followed the trail as it wound through towering pines that blocked the sun.

"Here. Lean on me," he said when she stumbled over a root. He could feel her exhaustion, the residue of her fear. Not waiting for an answer, he wrapped one burly arm around her waist. "Hang on, sweet thing. We're almost there."

When the trail narrowed and angled downward, he explained calmly, "I'll go first. Mike'll be right behind you. Don't worry."

She stumbled again as she heard the rising roar of the water below. The canyon wall was not nearly as steep there. It was strewn with boulders and an occasional clump of trees that partially hid the view, but Abby knew instinctively that the river was waiting below.

"No!" She jerked free of both men. "Don't make me go near the river. I won't go down there."

Jack stepped in front of her, blocking the sight of the drop with his body. "It's okay. Our camp is just below here."

"No!" She spun and clambered back up the trail,

her words thrown over her shoulder. "I don't believe you!"

The two men exchanged a quick glance. In three strides Jack was behind her. He grabbed her by the waist and held her as she struggled against him. "It's all right. Trust me."

"Let me go!" She pushed against him with her hands and head, trying to get away and back up into the safety of the trees.

"Sorry," he said, and lifted her up in his arms, trapping her against his chest.

She screamed, hit at him with her fists, kicked and struggled like a wildcat.

He just held her tight and half-walked, half-slid the rest of the way down to the river's edge.

At the bottom, his flock of tourists was waiting near his raft. Giddy from their own thrilling ride down the rapids and the unnerving sight of the girl in the water, they crowded around, worried and curious, knowing it could have been any one of them in her place. "How is she? Is she all right? Gee, *look* at her—"

"She's fine. Everyone go get some lunch," Jack commanded.

Abby heard the talk, the hush, the sounds of the others hurrying toward camp. Opening one eye, she peeked up at her rescuer. That determined little smile trembled on her lips. "I made a damn fool of myself, didn't I?"

"Hell, no. You were fine."

"Fine?" She blushed. "I was a wimp. Screaming. Crying. Oh, I never do anything like that, really. I just wish you'd never seen it."

"It doesn't matter—"

"It does to me." She released her hold on his neck and looked away. "You can put me down now."

He held her in his arms for another second, then set her down gently. "There's no reason to be embarrassed. It was a natural reaction; you were scared, wet, cold." He rocked back on his heels, studying her. "And you're *still* scared, wet, and cold. Let me get you some food, some warm clothes—"

"I can manage now. I'm fine. Really."

"Sure?" he asked, knowing better.

"Sure," she insisted.

He shook his head, grabbed his waterproof pack from the bottom of the raft, and led the way to camp.

"Do I look all right?" she asked, tugging her fingers through her hair.

"Why? Having your picture taken for the cover of *Vogue*?"

"*Sports Illustrated*," she teased back.

His grin lit the sharp planes and angles of his face.

For the first time, Abby really looked at him. He was exceptionally handsome, his face and body carved by sun, wind, and water into a harsh ruggedness. There was no slack to the man, no softness; even his eyes were the gray of rock, of granite. Dark brows, dark hair, dark glint in his eyes. But he had a Tom Sawyer grin.

"Thanks," she said, biting her lips. "Thanks for *everything*."

"You're welcome. I'm just sorry it ever happened. But take my advice and go easy on yourself this afternoon."

"Oh, I intend to. I'm going to take a walk in the woods, sit in the sun, read a book—"

"I was thinking more of a good, solid sleep: A shot of Scotch and out."

"But I'm fine. Really—"

Her words were cut short by a screech from across the bridge that spanned the river there at Renner's Ford.

"Abigail, oh, Abby! Are you all right? Oh, Abby, you had us so scared!"

Elaine came racing over the bridge, grabbed her,

and hugged her tightly. She was followed by the guide who had been responsible for the accident and the two young men from Estes Park. "Heavens, I didn't know if I'd ever see you again! Wasn't that awful? Terrible? We got out right away and then I couldn't find you and I didn't know what to do, and I kept imagining all these terrible things, but there wasn't anything we could *do*"—she glanced at her three companions for confirmation and raced on—"so we climbed up and followed the river, and my knees are all scraped, and I've got a thousand blisters, and then we saw you down there on the rocks. How *did* you ever get out of there? Jeff thought they'd have to call in a helicopter or something."

"*He* saved me," she said, turning her pale, heart-shaped face to Jack. "I—I don't even know your name."

"Jack Gallagher."

"Jack Gallagher," she repeated, feeling her throat close with stupid tears. She shook her head, blinking hard, and held out her hand. "I'm Abby Clarke, and this is my friend Elaine Shaw, and these are—"

He let go of her hand, finished with introductions. His pack was heavy, and he was hungry. *And* he had something to take care of first. "Excuse me. I've got work to do. And, Jeff—I want to *talk* to you." He led the other guide away, then turned and called back over his shoulder, "Take care of yourself, hear me?"

Abby nodded. She watched him stride away. There was dust in his dark hair, and his broad back was scratched and cut.

That's my fault, she thought suddenly, feeling again the slip of loose gravel, her rising hysteria. Sickness welled in her stomach, and the world spun.

"Are you okay?" Elaine demanded. "Gee, I bet you were scared to death! *I* would have died, just died! When we saw you across the river, I almost *fainted!* Didn't you hear us telling you to climb? We were screaming our fool heads off, and you didn't even try."

Abby stared at Elaine, her chest aching with her shallow, teary breaths. Good old feather-headed Elaine. Abby shook her head in disbelief. "I *couldn't*. I couldn't even move."

"Then how the heck did he get you up that rock wall?"

"He—he carried me."

"Wow! No kidding? Oh, I'd like to get my hands on that brawn!"

Abby turned away, away from the river, away from Elaine, away from the two young men in their wet khaki shorts and polo shirts. "I'm going to get some dry clothes from the van. I'll see you later."

"Yeah. Meet you at the food!"

Leaning against the door of the van, she wondered briefly if she had the strength to climb inside. But she knew it would be warm in there. Quiet. She pushed herself up and staggered down the aisle. In her backpack were a change of clothing, a sweater, socks, an extra pair of tennis shoes, a hairbrush. Hugging the pack to her chest, she made it out of the van and to a lean-to marked: "Ladies Only: Keep Out, You Bums!"

Inside the air was close, stifling. Without warning, her stomach coiled in a knot. In another minute she knew she'd be sick. Quickly, she pulled open the door and stumbled out.

Jack had been sitting on an overturned barrel with a cold beer in his hand, watching for her. Now he rose, waved the others back, and strode across the clearing. He caught her before she fell, and held her against his chest, cradling her gently. "Damn stubborn woman. I thought I told you to take it easy."

"I—I was just going to change my clothes."

"In there? I'd suggest you spend as little time in there as possible!"

"But—but—"

"Stop arguing with me."

That was all he said. Dark eyes flashing, he scooped her up in his arms and carried her up the path to a tent pitched in a circle of pines. Inside was a cot. He sat her on its edge and disappeared. In a moment he was back with a towel and a bucket of water. He waited while she splashed water on her face and neck, then washed her hands and arms, and splashed some more on her throat.

"Not feeling too good, huh?"

She shook her head. "I don't think I'm ever going to feel good again."

"You will, if you'll just listen to me. I'm talking from experience."

"Oh, you make a habit of rescuing drowning women?"

"I make it a habit to see no one needs to be rescued! No, I meant firsthand experience; the river's knocked me around a bit, too."

She looked up at him, too exhausted to ask questions. Everything ached. Everything hurt.

She just nodded in surrender.

"Here," he said, pouring amber liquid from a bottle into a dusty glass. "Drink this."

She did, and gasped as it burned a path down to her stomach.

"One more," he said, filling it again and handing it back.

Tears stung her eyes, but she drank it all.

"Good. Now get out of those clothes. I'll wait outside. And put on something loose and comfortable."

"But this is all I have," Abby whispered, pulling a T-shirt out of her backpack.

"Here." He fished in a trunk and came up with a huge faded sweat shirt. "Try this."

Her arms felt heavy as lead and her head was beginning to whirl, but she didn't dare disobey. She pulled off her wet and muddy clothes, including her

bra and panties, and slipped into his sweatshirt.
The heavy cotton hung in folds across her soft breasts
and narrow waist, its ragged lower edge coming all
the way to the middle of her thighs. She could see
that her legs were scraped and filthy, her knee caked
with blood and beginning to swell, but she couldn't
figure out what to do about it. Her feet were bare
and cut. She must have lost her shoes and socks in
the river—she couldn't remember. The liquor had
the world spinning; if she had to sit up for another
minute, she would faint.

Trying to keep the dirt off his bed, she leaned her
head down against his pillow.

All she wanted was the comfort of her own pine
bed, the boards polished smooth by her father's hand.
And her quilt made from squares of calico and
hopsacking, homespun and denim, and the one
square of her mother's wedding gown, yellowed now
but the satin so smooth, smoother than anything
she had ever touched as a child and therefore precious. She wanted it now. Needed to feel its warmth
and promise of safety. Needed to be held and loved—

"Ready?" Jack called from outside, scattering her
thoughts.

"Ready."

"Now," he said, filling the door of the tent with his
body, "sleep!"

"Ah, a man of many words." She laughed softly,
liking him for his directness, his strength.

"So I've been told." He grinned back. "Good night."
He stepped close and began to unfold a blanket.

"Oh, but I'm a mess! I'll get your bed dirty."

"It's seen worse." He tucked the covers up to her
chin.

"But where will you sleep?"

"You sure do know how to worry, don't you? How
the hell did anyone talk you into getting in that
raft?"

"I don't even know how I g-got talked into C-Colorado!"

she stuttered, her teeth beginning to chatter again. "Oh, no! What's happening? I thought you said I'd feel b-better."

"You will. Later. You'll probably feel worse for a while, but you've got to ease up and let it all out. There's no other way to get rid of that kind of fear. Here, I'll hold your hand for a while."

"Oh, you d-d-don't have to do that. I'll be fine." Tears ran down her cheeks. "I'm just cold. . . ."

"Damn stubborn woman," he said, and climbed into bed next to her. He wrapped his arms around her and pulled her up against him.

She rubbed her face against the front of his shirt. "What if this is a dream and I'm still down there?" she wailed. "Please—please save me."

He held her tighter, wrapped one hard leg around hers to stop her shaking, and stroked her hair. His hand was cool, his body warm and solid and wonderfully real. "It's all right," he whispered into the top of her hair. "All right, I'll save you."

He held her until she fell asleep.

Two

"Ow! Oh, no—ow!" Abby groaned, rolling over. Everything hurt, from her toes to the ends of her hair. She vaguely remembered a warm body next to hers, a pair of strong arms holding her, but now she was the sole occupant of the narrow cot. Trying not to move anything but her eyeballs, she peered around the dim tent: Empty. Outside a jay screeched, and the wind sang in the pines.

Suddenly all the aches and pains meant nothing. It was morning, and this morning was a present she had not expected to see. It was better than the rag doll in her Christmas stocking when she was six, the pink prom dress her mom had sewn and left wrapped in tissue on her bed. All the wishes and hopes and disappointments of her life faded against the golden light that filled the tent with dancing motes. Dust fairies, her mother had called them so many years ago. Dust fairies. Well, this morning she could believe in anything!

Stretching her arm out to touch the golden light, she flinched in pain. And when she sat up, the world did a quick little spin. Abby closed her eyes and counted to ten, fighting down the dizziness by sheer willpower.

"There, that's better," she assured herself, blinking to clear her vision. But things looked just as bad—worse, really: She was filthy; her arms and legs were scratched and caked with dirt, one knee raw and swollen; and her feet were grimy. All in all, she looked like the most woebegone ragamuffin to ever come out of Hooper, Florida!

Dismay quickly gave way to fear. The previous day swept back, with all its terrible memories: The water, the rocks, the cold, the panic. She felt her heart leap to her throat, her throat tighten with tears. She needed someone to hold her, to reassure her. But there was no one there who knew or cared how she felt. She was all alone.

Carefully she stood up and with trembling fingers reached into her backpack, pulled out her wallet, and opened it to the little plastic folder full of pictures. There was her mother's tired, steady, resolute gaze; her father's weary, loving smile. Seeing them, Abby drew a deep breath and reached down into herself for the strength that had carried through hard times before. With a stubborn lift of her chin, she pulled shorts on under the sweat shirt and pushed open the tent flap.

The first thing she saw was the upward sweep of mountain against an azure sky. The second was Jack Gallagher, straddling a fallen log, intent on the map in his hand. Her heart did a little flip. *See, girl, you're not alone; he was there watching over you.*

As he looked up, smiled, and walked toward her, Abby saw again the hard ruggedness of the man. And she saw, too, the power of his stride, the square cut of his jaw, the unwavering self-assurance of his gray eyes. Abby felt a shiver travel up her spine. This man could have come from another galaxy, he was so different from anyone she had ever known: Imposing, unnerving, bigger than life. There were no soft edges, no slow and easy southern ways to soothe her nerves. Instead he awoke a startling excitement in her.

"Oh, dear," she said, breathing hard. "Oh, my." Then, "Good morning!" she called loudly, with brave enthusiasm, staring at a point somewhere just to the left of his handsome face.

Jack Gallagher took one look at her, dirty, bedraggled, still half-asleep, and felt again that unexpected tightening in his gut. He thought he had slept it off. Thought it was just her helplessness, her needing him, her innocent courage that had him thinking crazy thoughts. But one look at her and here it was again, like a good right to the jaw. Crazy!

"Morning," he answered. He stopped a safe distance away, because he wanted to touch her. "How are you feeling?"

"Oh, I'm just fine now. Honest." She met his eyes and smiled. "Isn't it a gorgeous morning! I've never seen trees this tall. Or heard so many birds, or—"

"Or been so glad to be alive?"

"Yes, I guess that's it. Silly, isn't it?"

"Nope." Understanding flickered in his eyes. "I've had mornings like that. They're a present dropped on the foot of your bed when it isn't even Christmas."

Abby breathed in the cool mountain air. He knew! She wanted to tell him, *Yes, that's just how I feel, that's it: You've read my thoughts!* But she was too private a person ever to reveal that much to a stranger. Instead she steadied her wobbly voice and said, "One thing I'm sure of. I'll feel even better after a good hot shower. Can you point me in the right direction?"

"I can do better than that," he said, and grinned. "After all, I'm a guide with a reputation to uphold. Follow me."

"Wait. Just let me get my clean clothes." Ducking back inside the tent, she grabbed her pack. She debated putting on clean socks and tennis shoes, but her feet were so filthy she decided to wait until she had showered.

Jack was already a way down the path, and Abby had to trot to catch up. A small groan escaped her lips as she strained sore, aching muscles. "Ow!" she yelped, stepping on a sharp rock with her bare foot. Oh, where was the warm, sandy ground of home?

Jack turned. Cursing himself silently, then hurried back and took her arm. "Sorry. I thought you said you were fine."

"I thought I was!" With a rueful smile she added, "I guess there are a few bumps and bruises hiding under all this mud."

"Yup. After a spill like that, you usually find all kinds of aches and bruises the next day."

"Oh," she whispered, remembering. "I hate that river!"

He wrapped an arm around her trembling shoulders. "Hey, it's not the river's fault. You picked the wrong outfit, the wrong guide—"

"The wrong *vacation*, ho-ney!" she drawled, stretching her vowels with a down-home sultriness that made Jack grin. "I mean, I could've been bird-watching in the Everglades, or lying on the beach at Daytona, or—"

"Sounds dull."

"No, it sounds safe and sensible. And I'm a safe and sensible person." Their gazes held through a pause that was perhaps a heartbeat long, and then Abby added softly, "That's who I am, and I can't afford to be anything else."

Jack frowned. Without another word he led the way down a steep trail that just skirted the clearing and stopped in front of a hand-pumped shower rigged at the water's edge.

Abby skidded to a stop at his side.

"This is it?" she exclaimed, wide-eyed, breaking the tension.

"The Gore Canyon Hilton, at your service. You

wash, I'll pump." Jack handed her a blue terry towel from a hook nailed in the wooden wall. The wall itself came just up to her shoulder; there was no roof!

That dark, appraising glint flickered in his eyes again. "Hope you're not shocked."

For the first time, Abby laughed out loud, a sweet ringing peal of laughter that sailed to the tree tops.

"What's so funny?"

"It's just that I'm a country girl. I've taken many a bath in a galvanized tub set smack dab in the middle of the kitchen. No," she said, and grinned, "this doesn't shock me."

Abby tossed the towel over the side, then ducked inside, pulled off her clothes, and threw them across the wooden wall next to the towel. On tiptoe, she looked over at Jack. "No peeking," she warned, eyeing him warily.

"Scout's honor," he assured her.

Goose bumps lifted all over her bare skin. It was no boy scout on the other side of the wall—of that she was sure! Instinct warned her to get done and back into some clothes, *fast.*

"Soap?" she asked, looking around. All she saw was a piece of root stuck on a nail. "Don't *tell* me . . ."

"Yucca root. No pollution," he explained calmly.

"Should have known!" Shaking her head, she stepped under the shower head. "Okay!"

"Okay," he answered, and she heard the creak of the pump handle and got hit right over the head with a gush of ice-cold water. "Yikes! Turn on the hot!" she yelled, laughing even as she did, knowing this was it.

She hadn't washed as fast since her childhood in Hooper.

Covered with suds, she peeked over the wall to make sure he was keeping his promise, and sure enough, she saw the chiseled line of his profile. But she thought she detected just the faintest hint of a grin lifting the corner of his mouth.

She scrubbed faster, sticking separate, goose-bump-covered parts of her anatomy under the icy spray. "Enough, enough!" she shouted finally, rinsing the last of the lather out of her hair. "Stop!"

Abby toweled off, delighting in the luxury of clean hair, clean skin, clean clothes. Rubbing her hair dry, she hummed a little song to herself as she stepped out from behind the partition.

Jack's dark eyes widened in surprise. She was a golden girl, a slender woman painted in a palette of summer colors: The gold of her skin, sun-streaked blond hair that lifted and curled as the wind dried it, touches of coral at cheeks and lips, and those sky-blue eyes. He whistled softly between his teeth. "Sure am glad the river only gave you a few bruises and left the rest untouched!"

Abby blushed, the blood rising to her cheeks so quickly, it made her dizzy. She pressed one hand to her throat and felt her pulse fluttering wildly beneath her fingertips.

Jack reached over and put his hand gently on top of hers. "Hey, I'm sorry! I keep forgetting what you just went through. But don't worry, I'm a rough-talking river rat—"

"A *wonderful* river rat who saved my life!" she insisted fiercely, reaching up to touch his unshaven cheek.

They both felt the sudden jolt of electricity. For only a second, Jack recklessly considered taking advantage of her vulnerability: He'd sweep her up in his arms, cradle her slender warmth against his body, carry her back to the tent, and make fiery love to her. Then he saw the confusion in her wide eyes and put a hard rein on his desire.

Abby, equally as flustered, quickly changed the subject. "How about some breakfast? *Your* treat," she added teasingly. Her usual reserve seemed to have fled, banished by the wonder of the warm sun, the solid, wonderful earth beneath her feet, and this man.

This *was* an extraordinary day, something good coming to balance the bad, as her mother always said. And if it didn't seem so safe and sensible, and if she didn't know quite how to handle it, well . . . it was only for one day. She'd wing it!

Still laughing, Jack cupped her elbow with his broad hand. "Come on. I want to get a bandage on that knee of yours, and I'll introduce you to the rest of the crew."

The rest of the "crew," as he called them, were gathered in the clearing down near the riverbank, sitting on logs or upturned barrels, drinking coffee, playing poker, or studying U.S. geological-survey topographical maps of the rivers. The maps were creased and worn, stained with coffee, covered with large *X*'s and dates penned in indelible ink. Their voices were a muted whisper against the roar of the river beyond.

A bearded giant of a man looked up as Jack and Abby emerged from the woods. "Hey, you river rats, straighten up! Here's the boss—with company."

"Abby Clarke, my partner, Bear Dempsey."

"Glad to meet you," Abby said, staring as her hand vanished in the man's grip.

Bear introduced her around while Jack went for the first-aid kit and a mug of steaming black coffee.

There was an older man, sixty, perhaps, with a white scar down his cheek; two women, lean and sunburned and athletic-looking; and several men in denims and cut-offs and T-shirts: guides, rafters, kayakers—river rats all.

They'd look up for a moment and nod politely, offer a name or more often a nickname, Scratch or Lucky or Debby Dare, and return to their own business. There was an intensity here that Abby felt familiar with. It was the singleness of purpose, the camaraderie that she had seen between her father and the grove workers on the nights that frost threatened. Charting the cold front, readying the smudge pots, they had given the tourist, the curiosity seeker, the same cool welcome she now felt.

It didn't bother her at all. She sat on the edge of a log and nursed her coffee. Jack had stopped to peer over someone's shoulder at a worn, creased map. She overheard snatches of their conversation: "The Dolores River . . . Snaggle Tooth Rapid . . . Class Five . . . portage." It all sounded terribly ominous, but Jack laughed. "Yup, that's a sure case of rapid fever!"

"What's 'rapid fever'?" Abby asked as Jack hunkered down beside her, his hands resting on his denim-clad thighs.

"It's when you take one look at a rapid and your stomach hits your throat. Best thing to do is portage."

"But *do* you? Do you carry your raft—or ride it?"

"Depends on how high the water is. How fast. How good I'm feeling."

"I could never feel *that* good!" Abby swore. "From now on, if it's not a lake, it's too high, too fast."

He laughed. "You'd get used to it."

"Not me." She took another sip of coffee and looked up the slope into the woods. "That's for me. Hiking. Walking. Sitting!"

"Climbing?"

"Like yesterday? On mountainsides, with ropes and falling rock? No, thanks." She looked at him out of the corner of her eye. "Do you?"

" 'Fraid so."

"Thought so," she muttered beneath her breath. "The man *must* be crazy!"

Jack heard and bit back a grin. "Sit still now," he commanded. "I'm going to put some iodine on that knee and wrap it for you."

Abby acquiesced, soothed by the good, strong coffee and the sure, strong touch of his hands. Someone else handed her a doughnut, and she nodded her thanks and wolfed it down in three bites. She hadn't had anything in her stomach but river water for longer than she cared to remember. Oh, for one of her gram's sweet sticky buns, crusted in pecans they had shelled themselves, sitting knee to knee on the big swaybacked porch under the magnolia trees . . .

Jack glanced up from his bandaging and caught her licking her fingers, a faraway look clouding her eyes.

"Hello, there," he said softly, filled with an irrational desire to have her look at him that way. "Whatcha thinking about?"

Pulled back from her daydream, Abby shrugged. "Just lazing around and letting you do all the work." She smiled.

He remained still for a moment, one hand resting on the bare skin of her thigh.

Abby read the flicker of desire in his eyes and decided it was time to change the subject again. "Any chance you've seen Elaine this morning?"

"Yup," he answered, straightening. "One of my guides took her and your two pals downriver in an oar boat. They left about nine—"

"What!" Abby choked, spilling coffee down the front of her shirt. "What? You let them get back on that damn river?" she shouted.

There was dead silence on the riverbank.

Then Bear got up, tossed his coffee on the ground at his feet, and stomped away. The others looked expectantly from her to Jack and back again.

He stood stiff-backed, tight-jawed for a moment, and then grabbed her arm and propelled her back up the path.

"What are you doing?" she demanded, squirming in his grip.

"I'm getting you out of there before someone decides to chew you up and spit you out."

Abby gasped. "Me? What did I do?"

Jack stopped, took hold of both her shoulders, and turned her to face him. He knew he should let her go. See her get on the van back to town that afternoon and forget her. That was what was going to happen anyway, so why explain? It was crazy to try!

But she had already *said* he was crazy—and emotion he couldn't explain made him want to try, just this once.

His intense gaze swept from her sandy blond hair, to those clear blue eyes, to her stubborn, beautiful mouth. His expression grew thoughtful.

"I don't know if this will make sense, but if you're willing to listen, I'm willing to try." He waited for her to nod, then continued. "We, the people you just met and I, we love the rivers. Not just the Colorado, but the Yampa, the Piedra, the Gunnison, the Blue, the Dolores. We love the canyons, with their wild names: Desolation, Cataract, Animas, Split Mountain. For us, the rivers are adventure and sport, risk and challenge. They're what we test ourselves against, the things we use to measure our lives. They fill us with excitement, with passion."

He placed his hands gently around her face and tilted it up to his. "Tell me, what fills you with passion, Abby Clarke? What do you love?"

"You are crazy," she whispered. "You don't even know who I am, where I come from, what I do for a living—"

"We'll get back to that. Answer my question."

But she stood silent, mesmerized by his touch. Pictures flashed unbidden behind her eyes: Acres of orange groves, the sultry Florida air heavy with the scent of orange blossoms; the shabby, unpainted house of her childhood; her parents; a corncob doll; an old hound waiting on a dusty road. These were things too personal to share. But there must be *something*; she owed him that—and more. *So, Abigail Jean, what can you tell this man?* Up popped the image of her neat little restaurant, with its yellow shutters, and the Open for Business sign in the window.

Jack saw the smile form on her lips, washing away the haunted look her lovely face had worn. He waited silently, wondering, one thumb absently circling on the cool skin of her cheek.

"My restaurant," she answered with great surety.

"A . . . restaurant?" he echoed skeptically, frowning.

"*My* restaurant," she said insistently. "My *own*. I built it from nothing, just an idea, a dream, and now people come from miles around, from Eustis and Tavares and—" She stopped suddenly and gave a pixieish smile. "You wouldn't know any of those places, not a one. But it doesn't matter, because *I* know them, and back there, they know me. That's home. You asked, and I told you—but I don't expect you to understand." She set her hands on her hips, cocksure and defiant.

"You didn't give me a chance to understand. Lord, you are a short-tempered woman."

"So I've been told," she said, echoing his words of the night before.

He gave a shout of laughter, narrowed his eyes, and grinned at her. "Well, you gonna try me?"

Lifting one shoulder in a little shrug, she matched his grin. "Maybe. Why should I?"

"Because I want to know something about you. I *have* to! According to an old Indian legend, once you save someone's life, a part of that person stays with you forever. Well, you wouldn't want me to carry a total stranger around in my heart for the rest of my natural days, now, would you?"

Abby swallowed hard.

"Okay," she conceded, smiling. She walked over and perched on a boulder, arms wrapped around her knees. "Well, I own a restaurant in Mount Dora. That's central Florida, just north of Orlando. Disney World, you know? It's really nice: Lovely, and quiet—intimate. I call it the Paradise Café. And I'm one *terrific* cook! I opened it four years ago with every cent I could save and borrow and beg, and it's done well, knock wood! I mean, sometimes—well, sometimes I can't believe it myself. But the whole area's growing, and suddenly I'm not in the sticks any more; I'm 'fashionably removed from the city's hubbub'—or so says my advertising!"

Now that she'd started she couldn't stop, and the words tumbled out. "And recently I took on a partner who's got money to invest, I mean the kind of money I could *never* get hold of, and we're going to expand and redecorate, and we'll reopen on Memorial Day weekend, and it's going to be wonderful! So there it is." And, her eyes glowing with pride, she laughed as if it didn't matter what he thought.

"Nice," he said. "Sounds nice. And I'll be careful never to say anything bad about your restaurant."

Abby dropped her gaze, ran her fingers through her curls, and grinned ruefully. "Ah." She sighed, folding her hands in her lap and looking away back down the path. "I see your point. Well, that's a nice—an *acceptable* river you've got there."

He came and knelt beside her. "Can we try for 'fantastic'?"

"Don't push your luck."

Another husky laugh rumbled in his chest. "Okay, let's go on back and I'll square you with the crew." He rose and held out a hand.

Abby slipped hers into the pockets of her shorts. "I don't think so, Jack. I didn't mean to offend anyone, but my apologizing won't make any difference. Besides, I'll never see any of them again, so their opinion of me doesn't matter too much, does it?"

Jack felt a strange constriction in his chest. He dropped his hand, but stood nailed to the ground. "Any chance you'd want to stay another day? Give that knee a chance to heal?"

"And get into even *more* trouble? No, I don't think so!" She shook her head, sending her hair flying around her flushed cheeks.

"But your pal seems to want to stay—"

"Then let her! Anyway"—Abby sighed—"we're not such pals. She works in a little boutique nearby, and when she heard I was closing for the remodeling, she talked me into this vacation." Lifting one shoulder in a tiny shrug, she continued. "I haven't had too much experience with vacations; never could afford one or find the time. And Elaine made Colorado sound so exciting, I just—Well, I got caught up in it. I told you, I never take chances like this."

"Then I owe her some thanks," Jack said, leaning over her, his voice a husky rasp.

Abby's huge eyes flew to his face. Her cheeks were flushed. She knew in a moment he was going to kiss her, and that it would be like no other kiss she had ever tasted. For a second she waited in breathless anticipation, but then common sense hit her like a bucket of cold water. This was crazy! More risk! More danger!

Pressing one hand firmly against his chest, she shook her head. "I think I'd better go lie down. The world's spinning."

Jack wanted to argue, but he held his tongue. The rivers had taught him this: Oppose the current and it would fling you out of its path. But learn its depths and turns and nature, and then you could ride it to heaven.

All he needed was time and patience, yet this blue-eyed girl with her soft southern drawl was snatching both away. He wanted her. Without knowing her, without knowing why, he knew that much! And he was a man used to getting what he wanted.

But Abby was already moving away up the path. "Is it all right if I borrow your bed again for a while? My knees are starting to give way." She was careful not to look back. And without waiting for his answer, she disappeared into the tent, leaving him standing there.

• • •

After a short nap, Abby spent the rest of the morning and early afternoon in a glade in the forest. She could still hear the roar of the river and catch a glimpse of figures moving along its bank, but she carefully averted her eyes from every glimpse of Jack Gallagher. It was pointless. She was not going to risk getting involved, not going to risk anything! The things that mattered, the things that were possible, were waiting back home. There was no sense breaking her heart over something she couldn't ever have—like that shiny, red ten-speed bicycle years ago. She was older now, wiser now. So she looked carefully, stubbornly away from Jack Gallagher.

She leaned against a Ponderosa pine, her sketch pad on her lap, a good mystery in her pack on the ground next to her. Safe, solitary occupations. The sun slid through the branches, shifting the shadows slowly. After a little while, her heart slowed its wild flutter, and her aching muscles relaxed.

She must have drifted back into sleep, because the next thing she heard was the rattle and rumble of the van winding down the dirt road to the camp.

Getting up, she winced at the stiffness in her arms and legs, gingerly brushed herself off, and headed slowly down to the long ride back to Estes Park, her motel room, and, eventually, home.

When Abby reached the camp, Elaine and her two beaus were standing in the middle of the clearing, gulping cold beer and laughing. They looked none the worse for the day's raft trip. In fact, they were wide-eyed with excitement.

Elaine had a red bandanna tied jauntily around her neck. She yelled and waved as Abby appeared. "Oh, honey chile, you missed the most wonderful ride! It is *amazing* what a real guide can do with that little rubber raft. We just *flew* down that river today." She paused and flung an arm around Abby's sore shoulders. Abby winced. "You're not mad at us for going without you, are you? Your Sir Galahad, there, said he didn't think you'd want to go, and you were still sleeping when we left—"

Abby blushed, her gaze sliding quickly to Jack and back again. "No, Elaine, he was right. I wanted a day to relax. But I'm glad you had a good time—"

"And tomorrow Tom and Bobby want us to go hiking with them. They know a wonderful trail in Rocky Mountain National Park. It goes right up to a waterfall. Sound good?"

"Not for me," Abby replied, shaking her head at her friend's unbounded enthusiasm. "I plan to be on the first plane to Florida."

"Oh, rats," Elaine said, pouting. Then she shrugged. "Well, maybe you'll change your mind. Come on, I guess we're ready to go." The driver had arrived and was climbing into the van.

Several other people, who had been in a different raft the day before, came down the path and climbed into the van after Elaine, Tom, and Bobby. Abby followed them.

She had one foot on the first step when she felt his broad hand on her shoulder. She turned, leaned back against the van's warm metal exterior, and met Jack's eyes.

"So?" he said softly. "*Will* you change your mind?"

Abby felt her heart knocking against her ribs. "No," she said. "I can't."

"But that's not fair. Now I know a little bit about you, and you don't know anything about me."

"I know you saved my life, and I'll always be grateful," she said.

"Gratitude is not what I'm looking for," Jack answered, leaning a hand against the van behind her, his body curving close to hers. His breath ruffled her hair. "Listen, I'm six two; a hundred eighty to a hundred ninety pounds, depending on whether I've been doing my own cooking. I'm thirty-five, not married, never been married, didn't think I was ever going to *be* married, but I took a look at you sleeping last night and thought, 'What will it be like to be married to this woman?' Now, will you stay another day?"

Not a word would squeak out of her throat. Abby shook her head.

"Why not?" he demanded.

"Because—because it doesn't make sense. One day—one more day . . . it's all impossible—"

"I *like* tackling the impossible."

"Well, I don't! No—I've got to get home."

"Stay and take a chance."

"I don't take chances. I don't take risks. Life is hard enough without them! No, I am a sensible, sane per-person—" His grin shattered the thread of her logic, and she stumbled over her words and sighed. "You just don't believe me because you've seen me at my worst."

"Darlin', if this is your worst, I'm in real trouble!"

Abby put both hands flat on his chest and pushed, but couldn't budge him. Instead she felt his heart pounding beneath her palm, the heat of his body burning her hands. She dropped her hands to her sides and stared at her feet. "Let me go, Jack. Please."

"Okay. But I'll be in town at the High Pines Lodge all day tomorrow if you do change your mind. And don't worry about lunch. I'll let you cook!"

Three

The High Pines Lodge straddled a pine-covered slope of the foothills, with boulders and loose scree taking the place of a front lawn. The mountains loomed behind.

Abby leaned out the cab window, tipped her head back, and slid her eyes all the way up to the top. Whew. Too big, too fierce. It scared her. *He* scared her. The trouble was, it was all mixed up in her head: The mountains, Jack Gallagher, the attraction of such wildness, and the fear of it.

Grab a plane, girl! Be smart. Be sensible.

Abby slid back onto the vinyl seat and rolled up the window. "I've changed my mind. Take me back to the motel and then on to the airport instead."

"The *airport*, miss? Which airport?"

"Denver. And hurry."

"Sure. It's your money." The tires kicked up gravel as the driver spun the wheel.

"Oh, wait! Stop!" She clutched her purse. *Money.* How much money? How much money had she already thrown away? She tipped forward and craned her neck to see the little meter anchored on the front dash.

"That's seventeen-fifty, miss. To here. And Denver would run you another fifty, easy."

She was no longer listening. "Seventeen-fifty?" She gasped, mentally adding the barest tip possible. "That's—that's more than three cases of canned peaches, six pounds of fresh swordfish, twenty cans of tomato puree—institutional size!"

"Look, if I ever want to go into the wholesale food business, lady, I'll give you a call. Now all I want to know is, do you want to go to Denver, or not?"

"Not! Definitely not! And don't you dare drive this thing another *inch* with me in it!" she added, as he shifted back into first.

"I was just going to take you back to the front door—"

"I'll walk. Thank you." She snapped open the door, stuck one foot firmly on the ground, and dug a twenty out of her wallet. She looked at it, frowned, and reluctantly handed the money to the driver. "Thank you very much."

"Yup. Enjoy your stay."

"Ha! That's like telling a lobster to enjoy his last swim—as you put the lid on the pot!" Abby said, but no one was listening.

The wind sang in the pines and tugged at the hem of her skirt. To her left came the rat-a-tat-tat of a woodpecker. She looked off into the woods, carefully avoiding the sight of the low, rambling inn, its stone facade, and wide wooden porch.

"Hi!" came a shout from the porch, along with the sharp slam of the screen door. Jack was leaning against the wooden railing. "I was watching for you. For a minute I wondered if you were coming or going."

"I'm going," she answered back quickly, still facing away but catching a glimpse of him out of the corner of her eye. Even that one glance was enough to set her heart pounding.

"Don't go," he said, grinning. He was wearing jeans, and his shirt sleeves were rolled back over his forearms. "Come on in," he coaxed.

"No. I shouldn't have come." She turned and started down the path. "There's a plane at seven tonight, and I'm going to be on it. So good-bye, thanks again, and—"

"And what? 'See you around'? I won't. *We* won't."

That brought her to a halt, her heart jumping like a bean in a skillet. But she kept her back to him. "I guess that's the way life is sometimes," she said, soft but stubborn.

"I guess I can live with that," he answered.

Abby felt the heat of his gaze like a hand lifting the hair at the back of her neck. She just had to turn around.

He stared at her a moment, his eyes narrowed, then shook his head. "Nope. I'm wrong. I *can't* live with that. Won't. So come on in here. Let me introduce you to Pop. Show you around. We'll cook us some lunch and take a walk and maybe go somewhere for dinner."

"Lunch, that's all! Don't you be making any big plans! And then you've got to give me a ride back. I haven't got money to throw away on cab fare like this. Honestly, why didn't you *warn* me how far out you lived? This cost me a fortune!"

"I'll make it worth your while. Come in," he said. When she hesitated, he added coaxingly, "Come on. You're here already. There's nothing to be scared of."

She laughed, nervous and excited at the same time. She should go. Now. Why, any other man she'd just walk away from. But Jack Gallagher was not any other man.

"Well?" he said, teasing, not asking. He simply held the door open and smiled that slow, irresistible smile of his.

The lodge was not at all what she might have imagined. No antlers mounted on the walls, no buffalo heads and gun racks. Instead there were hand-hewn beams; rough textured, beautifully designed

Navaho rugs; shelves of glittering geodes and crystals; and maps and photographs framed and hung on the whitewashed walls between windows that framed a scene more breathtaking than any painting. She could see the tops of the pines bending and swaying in the unheard wind. A Steller's jay, bouncy and bold as a puppy, hopped up a ladder of limbs and swooped into the sky.

Abby turned in a tight circle, her eyes shining. "Oh, this is beautiful! I could have been happy staying here, and I thought I had seen everything there was to see in Colorado."

"And that's close to the truth!" A wiry old man, thin as a butter knife, pulled himself up off the overstuffed sofa. His pale blue eyes crinkled with laughter as he held out his hand. "So you're the gal with the restaurant down near Disney World? Well, I'm real glad to meet you."

Smiling back, Abby reached out to shake hands, registering the fact only as they touched that there were just two fingers on his hand. Her eyes widened in surprise, and she took a quick little swallow, looked quickly around the room, and nervously started talking. "What a lovely room! I guess I expected elk heads all over the walls, but that's a beautiful collection of crystals and—Well, it's a pleasure to meet you also, Mr. Gallagher."

"Gallagher? One Gallagher in this neck of the woods is enough!" He winked, including her in his laughter. "Name's Stout. Nathaniel Stout. Makes me laugh each time I think on it. But you can call me Pop. And now, since it's the cook's afternoon off, I'm goin' in to fix lunch." And with that he hobbled stiff-legged into the kitchen.

"Wait!" she called, glancing quickly over at Jack.

He was watching her with a smile that barely curved his lips, but his dark eyes were shining.

"Hey, I thought *I* was doing the cooking," Abby said with a fierce frown of disapproval. "Paying my debts, making amends, etcetera, Jack."

"Far as I'm concerned, we're more than even. Your being here takes care of everything."

She felt the heat climb from across her breasts, up over her throat, to her face. A little sigh of exasperation—or was it arousal?—escaped between her parted lips. "Jack," she began, her voice soft and wistful, "there's no sense in it. None."

"I know."

"So?"

"So *what*, darlin'? You want me to stop looking at you? Thinking about you? Wanting to walk over and touch you? Heck, you'll get that wish soon enough. For now . . . well, I've never been a very sensible fella. So I'll just keep looking, thinking, wanting—"

"I'm going in to help with lunch!" Turning on her heel, Abby fled into the kitchen.

Jack followed her. He stopped in the doorway, his arms crossed over his broad chest, seemingly content to watch her tie a towel around her slim waist.

"There, dressed and ready for action," she announced. "And, Pop, you've got a mutiny on your hands if you don't put me to work." She laughed, trying to cover her nervousness.

"Sure. You can fix a salad. There's rolls warming in the oven, my homemade blackberry jam in that crock, and Jack's got trout cookin' on the grill."

"A mess of trout!" Abby corrected, feeling her shyness disappear. "That's what we'd say in Florida. A mess o' trout. A mess o' peas, or grits with gravy."

"Is that the kind of stuff you serve in that restaurant of yours?"

"Oh, that—and swamp cabbage and 'gator tails."

Both men looked so startled that Abby had to laugh. "Don't you two turn your noses up. That's good turn-of-the-century Florida cooking we're talking about. I get *requests* for that dish!" She grinned as she reached for a cluster of garlic and began removing the paper-thin covering. "But actually, I'm experimenting with a whole new Florida cuisine. Knife?"

Jack handed her a razor-sharp cleaver, and she went to work. Her hands moved with mechanical precision and speed, leaving her thoughts free to fly. "You wouldn't believe the variety of fresh seafood the boats bring in: red snapper and pompano, shark, grouper, shrimp, scallops. And I make sauces from papaya, guava, avocado, carambola, litchi, and longan, limes, oranges, melons—many of those wonderful subtropical fruits grow right in my own state!" She grabbed a bunch of green onions, stripped them down to the crisp inner stalks, and kept on chopping. "And a man I know, a neighbor from over near Tampa, came up with the idea of growing edible flowers for garnishing. I mean, you *eat* them! Nasturtiums! Isn't that wonderful?" She was grinning from ear to ear, dimples decorating her cheeks, her eyes shining.

"If you're a goat," Jack teased, but softly, not wanting to break the spell. "You sort of like what you do, don't you?"

"It's my whole life," she answered, giving him the softest little smile, a smile made up of pride and stubbornness and regret.

Jack felt a fist close in his chest. His eyes darkened, as if shades had been drawn suddenly between him and the world.

Abby stared down at the neat pile of perfect, one-eighth-inch onion sections. So orderly. So simple. Pressing her lips together, she started to tear the lettuce into a large wooden bowl.

Pop couldn't stand the sudden thicker-than-wet-wool tension in the room. "So, little gal, did your momma teach you to cook?"

It was so far from the truth, it made her laugh. Pressing her hand to her mouth, she shook her head. "My mother? She'd put a mess o' beans up in the morning, with some greens, and go out to work the groves with my father. There were seedlings to nurse, grafts to worry over, machinery to oil, canker and drought—and always a freeze on the way. Whenever they got back to the house, that's when dinner was. . . ."

Her voice drifted off, stolen away by the power of her memories. When she found it again, it was hushed, solemn. She drew a little breath. "No, my mother didn't teach me to cook. But in high school —in the library—I discovered cookbooks. I read them like romances, late at night, dreaming over them. Maybe because I was always hungry, hungry for the taste of something new, something exotic, something" —she caught her lower lip between her teeth, her blue eyes lit with visions—"something *delicious!*"

Jack could almost see that high-school girl, blond hair bouncing on her shoulders, dreaming her future. "So you decided to be a world-famous chef—"

"Don't y'all make fun of me," Abby insisted, pressing a fingertip to his lips.

"I wasn't," he whispered against her skin, the heat of his mouth searing her fingertip, racing up her arm to her heart.

She snatched her hand away and tucked it in the folds of the towel. "Anyway, I won myself a scholarship to Florida State, got a degree in business, and worked nights and weekends at Dunkin' Donuts. I still bake doughnuts in my sleep! Then I got a job with Holiday Inn. I started as a fry cook and ended up restaurant manager."

"Sounds like hard work—" Jack began sympathetically.

"Of *course* it was hard work!" She looked at him as if he were crazy. "Since when is making a living, getting ahead not hard work?"

"It depends on what you call 'getting ahead,' " he said in that maddeningly calm, husky voice of his. "If you mean wanting things, and sweating and saving to buy them, and then wanting more things, then I guess hard work is—"

"I *mean*, Jack Gallagher, wanting a better life than

the one you had yesterday. Being able to afford a home, and putting dinner on the table, and making sure the people you love don't want—that's what I mean. And none of it comes easy! And"—she reached up to poke his broad chest with one trembling finger—"I don't see you living in a tent or a shack. This looks pretty comfy to me! And if *you're* not working for it, someone is—or did!" She turned sharply to Pop, looking for confirmation.

"You're fishin' in the wrong waters, gal. You just don't know Jack Gallagher."

Before she could even squeak out a protest, Jack slipped one hand behind her back and pulled her off to the corner. He put his arms around her. "I bet it's been hard."

She couldn't answer—could barely stand. His chest was so solid, warm, and hard, a wall to lean against, a place to rest. And the heat of his body so close melted her, left her trembling. When she found her voice, it was weak as custard. "Oh, please—*please* don't be nice. On top of everything, don't be sweet and understanding. It's bad enough that—that—"

"That what?" he whispered down into her hair.

She spoke softly into his shirt, her face turned against his shoulder. "That you make me feel all kinds of things I don't want to feel. Can't feel. I'll never see you again, and it will be so much easier to leave angry."

"And what if I won't cooperate?"

She fetched up a little smile. "That's okay. I seem to be doing a good job of it all by myself."

They both laughed.

"Good!" Pop said from near the sink. "Now that the bell's rung for round one, could we get back to work, young'uns? The paying customers'll be down in a minute, their stomachs growlin'."

After a few minutes of clanging and banging around the kitchen, the salad was dressed, the rolls tucked in their basket, and a pitcher of iced tea poured.

Leaving it all on a rolling cart for Jack, Pop slipped an arm around Abby's shoulders and guided her into the dining room. "Jack tells me you had a rough day on the river."

"I've had better days," she said, and grinned, grateful to him for his tact and kindness.

"Well, the rivers can be harsh masters." He nodded sympathetically. "Here, you sit at the head of our table."

Already seated, looking hungry and cheerful, were a few of the "paying customers": a husband and wife from Kansas City and newlyweds from down in Denver. All the other guests had taken box lunches and disappeared after breakfast, scattered to hikes and trail rides and scenic drives through the national park. There were introductions and chatter, and then the food arrived.

Abby took a little bit of everything as the dishes went round, hoping she looked a lot calmer than she felt. Jack, Pop, the lodge itself had her head spinning. When Jack caught her eye, she smiled and looked quickly away, feeling as transparent as glass and hating herself for it. Her heart was pounding.

But the familiar magic of food won her over. Soon she was eating away happily, savoring tastes, collecting little bits of information for that recipe file in her brain. "Pop, you used honey instead of sugar in this jam of yours, didn't you! Ummmm. And, Jack, did you cook the trout over mesquite? It tastes something like that—but there's a flavor—" She took another nibble, lifted her shoulders, and closed her eyes, concentrating so hard that little lines showed between her golden brows. "I give up. Tell me!"

"It's ironwood." He laughed at her, his voice held low for her alone. "Now I know what to get you for Christmas!"

Laughing herself, she leaned over and put her hand on his arm without thinking. But then she took it back, and was more careful during the rest of lunch.

But she couldn't keep her eyes off him. And she couldn't keep Jack from watching her. She felt his gaze like a lingering touch on her hair, her cheek, her lips. It made all her skin feel hot. She could barely swallow, barely breathe.

When the guests excused themselves, the three of them lingered at the table. Pop was saying something about a daredevil kayak ride through some canyon, and Abby snatched at it, grateful for anything that would turn the spotlight safely back on Jack. "Come on, Jack, tell me about it!"

Jack just shook his head. "It was years ago; not worth talking about."

The old man laughed. "Jack, he does things for the doing, not the telling. He's like me. A rebel. Me, I loved planes. Flew mail in Alaska, walked on wings above county fairs, jumped out of planes just for the pleasure of being allowed to get back in. Even cropdusted, back in the days when we worked with those poisons bare-handed, shoveling the stuff into the bellies of the planes and kickin' a clump loose with our feet if it got stuck. That's why I'm fallin' apart now. Fingers first, then this old leg of mine . . ." He whacked his leg hard with a serving spoon, making Abby jump. "Wooden," he said, laughing, forbidding her look of horror.

"No need to look sad, little gal. I lived the life I wanted, and then, when I was startin' to wear down, I met Jack up in Wyoming. He was fresh out of college, doing some geology work and chompin' at the bit. I knew right away he had some of that same wildness in him, like me. He'd broken his collarbone kayaking down some river—remember, Jack?—and I told him if he wanted to see *rivers* he'd better get to Colorado before he got himself killed. And Jack, he knew I was asking for help even if I was too proud to come out and say it."

"Pop—" Jack frowned and shook his head, but the old man wasn't going to be stopped mid-say.

"Yup, he took my run-down old cabin and turned it into this place. He built it with his bare hands so's I could own somethin' worthwhile for once in my life. Now he's ended up takin' care of the place and me both, better than any son could've done." His eyes rested on Jack with so much open affection, Abby felt her throat close tight around tears.

Jack sat without moving a muscle, staring down at the tabletop. Pop cuffed him lightly on the shoulder and went on talking. "Hey, this here's what I wanted to tell. Jack—he loves the rivers the way I loved those planes. Ask to see his maps," the old man suggested, grinning.

"Pop, you show her your crystals. She doesn't want to see any maps." Jack leaned back, finally released from the emotion of Pop's words. "Besides," he added, locking his hands behind his head, "she hates rivers."

"Colorado rivers!" Abby protested. "Fast rivers with rapids and holes and crazy people floating down them in tiny, breakable little rubber rafts and boats that look like matchsticks!"

Jack gave a husky laugh. "What other kind of rivers are there?"

"Oh, slow-moving lazy rivers that wind through mangrove swamps or between live oaks hung with beards of Spanish moss." Lacing her fingers under her chin, she smiled dreamily. "The Suwannee. The Wekiwa. The St. Johns and the Peace and the Withlacoochee. Don't they sound friendly—even with alligators sunning on the sandy banks?" She winked, making both men laugh, caught as they were in the spell of her charm.

Finally Pop insisted on doing the cleaning up, so Abby followed Jack outside. She sat down on the top step of the porch, arms around her knees, and stared across at the mountains. The wind, crisp and cool, lifted her hair, tossing it about her face in golden curls. Jack was sitting with his back against the roughhewn wood of the house, watching her.

She turned and caught him at it again. "Jack, stop looking at me like that!" She laughed, her cheeks burning.

A smile tugged at the corner of his mouth. "Like what?"

"You know like what. Just stop it."

"How else can I memorize your face, Abby? Besides"—he turned his glance to the mountains—"it's the same way I look at those peaks." He nodded at the far-off, snow-clad summits. "Or at a ten-mile stretch of wild water. There's something there that talks to my heart."

"Jack, don't," she pleaded. "Be nice. Talk about something else."

"Like what?"

"Anything. The lodge. Your rafting company—what do you call it? G & D White Water Rafting? Tell me about Bear Dempsey and how you became partners. Tell me about how long your season is, and how many tourists you take out, and how many fall in! Tell me anything, Jack. Tell me about the mountains—" She stubbornly turned her face away and stared out at the peaks. "Out there—that's where you belong."

"Hey, I'm not Grizzly Adams. I'm a very civilized kind of guy."

"Sure, you simply like to take chances, maybe get yourself killed." She tossed her head and sighed. "Anyway, I can't imagine you anywhere but here."

"Funny. I was thinking about taking a trip south."

Shaking her head, Abby laughed softly. "No, I can't see you in the South. Too big. Too tall. You need the mountains: Fourteen thousand feet for a backdrop. No, in Florida, you'd tower over the palms, frighten away the flamingos, stride from Tampa to Cocoa leaving sinkholes in your wake!"

"*Very* funny!" He moved over beside her and ruffled her hair. "And I thought you were the kind of person who hates exaggeration. Who likes to look at everything with an honest eye."

"But that is honest, Jack Gallagher. That's how I'll always remember you: Bigger than life. Swinging down over that cliff to rescue me, carrying me back up to the top as if I didn't weigh more than a sack of feathers—"

"You don't."

"I do!" She giggled. "Who do you think tastes all my cooking?" She lifted one shoulder in a girlish, flirtatious way, then froze. Letting both shoulders drop, she hid her face in her hands.

He pulled her close, wrapping one arm around her trembling shoulders. "What is it?" His voice was a harsh whisper, stirring the hair that fell across her cheek. "Talk to me, Abby!"

"That's the trouble," Abby said. "All of a sudden it's like I don't know who Abby is. Not out here. Not with you. Jack, I'm not some little college coed, all flirty-eyed and teasing. And here I am, giggling, playing the role. I'm twenty-nine, a grown woman with responsibilities and a business; a serious, hard-working person. That's all!"

"Maybe you're all that—and more."

"Maybe. But I just don't think this is the time or place to find out."

"Why not?"

"Because in"—she glanced at her watch—"four hours I'm going to be on a plane headed home, and you'll be here, running your rafting business, your lodge, your rivers, and I'll be in Mount Dora running my restaurant. That's the way it is."

Jack lowered his gaze to the soft flutter of pulse at her throat. He was so silent, so still, she wondered for a moment if he was counting her heartbeats.

Then without warning he curved his body toward her and pulled her into the circle of his arms. He caught her off balance and lifted her up, up and against him, and held her there as he let his shoulders drop back down against the porch floor. She was resting on his chest, her breasts flattened against his shirt, her face inches from his.

"This is no way to have a conversation, Gallagher."

"I'm tired of conversations. Remember, I'm a man of few words."

She saw the smile in his eyes. And then he was kissing her. His mouth brushed cool and firm against the velvet softness of her lips. "I can't let you go away. I won't."

A deep stirring of arousal softened her sadness. She kissed his face, his eyes, brows, mouth, chin. "There's nothing you can do about it, Gallagher."

"I'll make you forget Florida."

Abby leaned back against his arms and pointed at the sky. "You see that sky? In Florida it's endless, and the clouds roll over from the Gulf, tall as mountains piled on mountains."

He kissed her, drawing his tongue slowly up the hollow of her throat.

"Hear that bird? At home I have a mockingbird that sits in my own orange tree and sings every song that birds ever learned."

He kissed her eyelids, first one and then the other, with incredible tenderness.

"Feel that air?" she whispered, letting her arms circle his neck. "At home it's soft and balmy, scented with hibiscus and gardenia and jasmine. And it blows through the palmettos and touches your skin like a lover."

He kissed her mouth, sliding his hands over her skin, touching her gently, but with great passion.

Abby kissed him back, passionately, her eager, hungry mouth turning and turning to fit his, to taste his kisses, his heat, his sweetness. Breathless, she kissed his lips and slid her tongue into the corner of his mouth, along his lips. His kisses were fierce and demanding, and deep within her she felt desire rise and burn, hot as a flame.

But then reality tapped her on the shoulder. "Stop—no, Jack, really. We shouldn't. . . ." She struggled in his arms.

"Who says we shouldn't? Every damn inch of me says we should!"

"Me too!" she whispered, pressing against him for just one more delicious second. Then she sat up, drawing her knees to her chest and locking her arms around them. Her breath came in short little gasps. "That's how I know I shouldn't. Because I want to so much."

"Oh, great. What are you, a Puritan? Do you sleep on a bed of nails?"

Abby gave a shaky little laugh. "The last thing I want to talk to you about, Gallagher, is where or how I sleep."

On the far side of the house, the door slammed. Pop came around, carrying a pick ax over one shoulder. " 'Scuse me, folks, I'm taking one of the Jeeps and going up the peak to see what I can find. See you kids later."

He left silence in his wake.

Abby drew a slow, steadying breath. "Jack? Why don't you show me those maps Pop talked about?"

"No." He sat up and stared off across the mountains, his arms folded across his chest.

Abby frowned. "Why not? Obviously it's not a secret. Other people know about it—"

"Dammit, you're not other people. I don't know why the hell not—but you're not! You're special—and you *won't* like it."

"Good," she said, standing up quickly and smoothing the front of her skirt. "Right now I need something *not* to like. Or do you just want to drive me back?"

Silently he stood, took her hand, and led the way. In his room there was a stone fireplace, a heavy oak chest and his bed. The windows faced the peaks, and one wall was covered with maps. Abby recognized the maps of the rivers, the same kind the river rats had been studying back at their base camp.

"What do the pushpins mean?"

"The ones I've already run."

"And the different colors?"

He shoved his hands in his pockets and took a deep breath that stretched his shirt tight across the muscles of his chest. "Different degrees of difficulty for the rivers and rapids. Green is Class I: Novice. Small waves, clear passage."

"There aren't too many of those. What's red? You've got *plenty* of them."

He narrowed his eyes at her obvious sarcasm. "I told you you weren't going to like this."

"That's okay. So?"

He gave her a long, hard stare, with just a hint of a smile twitching at his stern mouth. "Red's Class V: Expert. Long and violent rapids, steep gradient. Extremely difficult."

"And this?" She popped a black pin out between thumb and forefinger and held it up like a challenge between them.

He regarded her with his dark, knowing eyes. "That is Class VI: Extraordinarily difficult—nearly impossible, and very dangerous."

"That's what I thought." She nodded and dropped the little black pin into his hand. Sighing, she gave him a bright, false smile. "That was *just* what I needed."

"Abby—" He reached for her hand.

"But if it wasn't enough, look at all these pictures." She pointed to a dozen small black-and-whites stuck on the wall. "Look at you, smashed and bashed, but always that same triumphant grin! Yup—"

"Cut it out!" he said with a growl, pulling her close. "I'm alive, aren't I? You bet I am!" Pushing his hands into the pale golden cloud of her hair, he tipped her face up to his. His fingers brushed the nape of her neck, and shivers went up her spine.

He stopped mid-kiss and wrapped her tightly in his arms. "Hey, something walk across my grave?" he whispered.

"Hush!" she yelped. "Don't you say that! Never, not even joking! Oh, you—you don't care anything about your life. You're willing to *risk* too much. *Dare* too much. You're crazy, and you make me crazy!"

"A little crazy may be good," he whispered, stopping her words with his lips.

She ran her hand lightly up his back and across his shoulders, feeling the heat of his body through his shirt. "Just, please, be careful."

"Stay, and I'll be careful."

Abby pulled away, startled into total seriousness. "What?"

"Stay."

"I can't," she said simply. "I have to go home. I *want* to go home. Oh, Jack, you really don't know me at all. I have my own dreams. Small ones. Attainable ones, if I work hard enough. And responsibilities: A mother, a father, a sister I'm helping to raise, God love her, two cats to keep safe from alligators. I can't stay. I wouldn't stay. I won't."

The word echoed in the room.

"Then we'd better get going." His voice had a rough, unexpected edge.

"Yes. We'd better." Abby turned and headed out of the room. "I left my bag in the kitchen." Jack followed her silently. She grabbed her bag and faced him, fighting to hold her voice steady. "You'll tell Pop good-bye for me?"

"Yes."

They hardly spoke on the ride back to town. Jack pointed out a peak in the distance and told her its name. He stopped for two deer that grazed at the edge of the road, a doe and her fawn. And Abby smiled, leaning out the Jeep door for a closer look, marveling at the dark, liquid eyes, the incredibly narrow legs that carried them away in perfectly matched leaps and bounds when Jack lightly tapped the horn. She thanked him for that, and for the day and lunch. . . .

"Tomorrow?" he asked when he pulled to a stop in front of her motel.

"I can't believe we got here so fast," she said, averting her face. "That cost me twenty dollars this morning!"

"Tomorrow?" he insisted.

"I'll be home tomorrow."

"Can't I drive you down to the airport?"

"No." She shook her head firmly. "Better not."

"Well—maybe I'll see you again."

Her eyes slid to his face, then quickly away; she was afraid he'd see the tears welling there. It was hard to talk, so she shook her head again, then grinned. "Nope. I doubt it. You've got rivers to run. I've got a restaurant to run." She slipped quickly out of the Jeep and slammed the door shut between them, then offered a little smile. "But it was fun—"

"No, it wasn't," he said, not moving. One arm rested across the back of the seat she had left empty. The other held hard to the steering wheel. He stared at her. Then, with a brash wave, he gunned the engine and was gone.

Four

"Red snapper. Avocado. Oranges. Jack." Feeling her heart give a little hiccup of unhappiness, Abby stopped gathering the ingredients listed on her recipe and leaned weakly against the pantry shelf. *Jack.* Her stomach was knotted like an old rag, and a dull pain spread outward from her heart. Oh, she missed him. Hardly knew him and missed him terribly. Now, there was a laugh!

Except she wasn't laughing. Instead here she was, standing in the pantry of the Paradise Café one week before her Memorial Day weekend grand re-opening, her arms full of groceries, but her heart empty.

I should have made love with him. I should have. I couldn't regret it any more than I do already, she thought. With a sigh she rested her cheek against the freshly painted wall. "At least I would have something to remember."

"Did I hear you say 'remember'?" her new partner grumbled, poking his head around the corner. "Don't tell me you *forgot* anything. It's impossible! You bought out half the farmers' market, and enough cans to feed an army."

"Simon," Abby said, laughing, "it takes food to run a restaurant."

"It takes more than food, love. It takes pizzazz. And it's a lucky thing I've got plenty of it, because you're beginning to look a bit worn. Shadows under your lovely eyes, frown lines around your pretty mouth . . ."

"Simon—"

"Ab-by—" Simon said mockingly, drawing her name out into an unpleasant singsong. "I thought a person was supposed to come back from a vacation relaxed and refreshed. You came back a grouch!"

"How can you say that? I came back to find you didn't do half the things you said you would. I've been working sixteen hours a day just to catch up!"

"I did plenty." Simon sneered. "Did you look in the backroom? We now have the best wine cellar in Lake County."

"But we don't *need* the best wine cellar in the county. We need table linens, janitorial supplies. . . ." Abby drew a deep breath, struggling for calm. "Listen, it's all about done now, so let's not argue. I don't want to argue, Simon. I want this all to work out." She gave her head a tiny shake to chase the fears away. *It* has *to work out*, she prayed silently.

"It's gonna be great!" Simon said, draping a limp arm over her shoulders. "Hey, I've got a meeting in Miami this afternoon. Want to lock up and fly down with me? We can have a late dinner. Put a little money on the dogs, watch a little Jai Alai, do a few parties. What d'ya say?"

Abby shrugged off his arm and stared at him in disbelief. "I just told you how much work there is to do. Aren't you going to stay and help?"

"Not a chance." He straightened his tie, smoothed back his hair. "I'm the money man, remember? That was the deal." Smirking, he sauntered out.

Abby stood for a moment, rolling her eyes and swearing under her breath. Then, shaking her head, she collected the rest of the ingredients and walked into the main kitchen.

The beauty of it, the sparkling newness, made her feel better immediately. She set everything out on the counter, then ran her hand over the gleaming stainless steel, the smooth golden butcher block. She touched the opalescent thickness of the Lucite chopping boards, the round, reassuring shapes of the mixing bowls, the homey nested stack of measuring cups.

"I've got to learn not to let him get to me," she vowed, her eyes lingering on the heavy, copper-bottomed pans hanging above the stove.

And the truth was, without Simon's money she couldn't have afforded a new skillet, let alone this kitchen. And this kitchen was the key to her dreams: The café a success, money coming in, bills paid off for her and her family, and maybe even a little something in the bank. It was security. It was a future.

"I'll make it work, I will! I'll bite my tongue and be patient."

And with that promise made, she got to work. Opening one door of the giant walk-in cooler, she took out the snapper. In moments it was filleted, seasoned, sauteed. She peeled, diced, minced, simmered, and a sauce materialized. She was humming now, thinking of nothing but the taste, aroma, and eye appeal of the dish she was creating. A quick taste and she was smiling, the worry lines vanishing from around her wide blue eyes, the color blooming on her cheeks again. She sang a couple of lines from a popular song, tapping out the rhythm with her wooden spoon.

And as if the world around her could sense her fragile peace, the sun popped through a rift of high white clouds and sent a sunbeam shining through the kitchen window. Outside a mockingbird sang. "Oh, I may not be rich or famous or lead a glamorous life," she said to herself, "but I sure can cook!"

The back door swung open, and a teenager wearing a pink T-shirt, blue jeans, and a pair of bright pink high-tops hurried in. "Hi, sis. How's it goin'? I haven't seen you for five minutes since you got back. Wow! the kitchen looks great!"

Abby laughed. "Now I know things are back to normal. Jeanette, I think a person could get hurt wearing jeans that tight—"

"Shoot, Abby," came the teenager's flip reply, "you sound just like Mom. But it's worse because you're so cute. You should be in these jeans, having a good time—"

"I am having a good time. Or was until a moment ago. My sauce is going to curdle."

"Your whole life is going to curdle if someone doesn't get you to stop working and have some fun. But you never listen to me."

"Nor you to me!"

"True. By the way, I assume El Creepo isn't here, right?"

"Simon?" Abby asked, frowning.

"Him! Geez, he makes me nervous. Always sitting around, scoping me from the distance, Yuck! I couldn't stand him for a partner."

"Well, Lee Iacocca didn't happen to answer my ad."

"Who?"

"Never mind." Abby waved it away, but she still looked worried. "He hasn't gotten fresh, has he?"

" 'Gotten fresh'? I don't think they've said that in a hundred years. But no, he hasn't made a move on me." She grinned. "He acts cocky, but I think he's really scared of you."

A horn blared outside. Pink high-tops flashing, Jeanette raced across the kitchen and stuck her head out the door. "Hokay! I'm comin'!"

"I thought you were alone—"

"Nope. Tige and Willy are with me. School's out early because of finals, and we're going on a picnic."

"So how did you do?"

"Hmmm?"

"On your exam, Jeanette! Did you pass?"

"Oh, yeah, I think so. I sure *hope* so! I'm already taking math in summer school. But anyway, I stopped by to see if maybe you could lend me a couple of dollars?"

"I thought you were working at the Seven-Eleven."

"I am. Was. They've had a temporary layoff. But don't worry, I put an app in at McDonald's and Burger King. Not playing any favorites." She grinned.

Abby sighed and shook her head at her sister's dauntless unconcern. But then, she was only a kid. And things were tough enough.

"Here." She reached into her pocketbook, then paused, holding the bill between her fingers like a lure. "Why don't you introduce me to your friends?"

"Sure." Jeanette laughed. "You'll love them." Shouting out the door, she waved them in, two boyish versions of Jeanette, long-haired, jean-clad kids with wide smiles and easygoing charm. They blustered in, bumping shoulders and shoving, causing Abby to fear for her chairs, glassware—even the stove!

"It's nice to meet you both. Tige?" she ventured, holding out her hand.

The blonder of the two gave it a rough pump. "Hi."

The second followed suit. "And I'm Willy. Nice to meet you. You know, my parents eat here a lot. They don't bring me 'cause they say I eat too much, but they really think you're a terrific chef."

Abby grinned, delighted, immediately impressed with this boy's fine upbringing. "Well, please tell them we're reopening on Friday and I'll be looking forward to seeing them."

"Sure. Well, we better get goin'."

"Have fun. And, Jeanette, be good. I'll see y'all soon—"

"Oh, that reminds me. Mom wants you to come for dinner. And she said, quote, 'If that girl says she's too busy, tell her she'd better at least show up for breakfast. She's working too hard.' Unquote." Having delivered the message, she evaporated through the door. Her friends followed.

"Tell her I'll try!" Abby called at their backs, and shut the door.

The sauce had congealed to a lump in the bottom of the pan. "Well," Abby said musingly, washing it in warm, sudsy water and already beginning to hum softly to herself, "let's see what happens this time if I add a little fresh lemon juice, some mango, and. . . ."

It was well after two o'clock when the phone rang. After wiping her hands on her apron, she grabbed the receiver. "Hello," she sang.

"Abby?"

Her heart stopped. She slapped her hand over the mouthpiece, hoping he hadn't heard the sharp intake of her breath or the crazy pounding of her heart. *Count to ten. Quick.* But she couldn't. She couldn't wait that long. "Jack?" It came out a whisper. A breath of hope, fear.

There was a low, husky laugh on the other end of the line. "Yup. How are you?"

"Fine." Her voice squeaked. Abby felt as if she had swallowed a hot potato that just wouldn't cool down. Tears stung her eyes, and her throat ached. "Jack . . . you shouldn't have called. It's silly. It's—it's—" She stumbled over the rush of emotions, then asked helplessly, "Why *did* you call?"

"Because I missed you. I want to see you again."

"We can't."

"You bet we can! I'm here. Come get me."

Dead silence. And then, softly, "*Where* are you, Gallagher?"

"Orlando International Airport, the sign says. That-away to Disney World! You want to come pick me up or should I grab a cab?"

"No."

"No what, darlin'?"

"No," she said, gasping. "Neither! Gallagher, get back on that plane and go home to Colorado. Home to your rivers, your friends, Pop—"

"It's you I want."

She felt dizzy with excitement. How was she supposed to think straight when the ground kept dropping away beneath her feet? "J-Jack—" she stuttered.

"Don't bother to argue. Or tell me how little sense this makes. I'm not leaving until I see you. So, if I start walking now, I should be there in about, oh, six hours. Seven if I stop for dinner."

"Stay where you are!" she shouted, and began to hang up. She yanked the phone back to her ear. "Wait! Where *are* you? What gate? What airline?"

"Continental. Gate forty-seven."

"Okay." She swallowed hard. "Wait there. I'm coming to get you."

She was trembling with a wild mixture of dismay and pleasure. Jack was here. In an hour she would see him. In an hour she could touch him, taste his kiss on her lips. . . . In an hour she was *supposed* to be perfecting the sauce for her snapper, going over next week's order with the seafood distributor, signing a contract with a new exterminating company, and meeting with Mrs. LaRue of the Tavares Garden Club, who wanted to arrange an awards luncheon for twenty-eight.

Her hands began to shake. "Jack Gallagher, I'll get you for this!" she swore. Her words echoed around the kitchen and came back to mock her. That was exactly what her heart was telling her to do: Go get that man! And now!

The highway was a bright white ribbon unwinding in the bright white glare of a Florida afternoon. It led her south down the old Orange Blossom Trail, past lakes and rolling hills, replanted groves dotted with tiny green trees, deserted groves with their bare brown skeletons, small towns about to be gobbled up by Orlando's eager growth, tile-roofed suburban shopping centers, industrial parks, topless bars and fast-food chains, and then to the airport.

Following the color-coded signs, she took the ramp marked Arrivals and slowed as she approached Continental. She scanned the drive for a parking spot, and had just found one down the way when Jack came striding out through the double wide doors into the bright white sunlight.

She saw him lift one arm to shade his eyes while he found her again, and then his face broke into a grin.

It made her heart stop . . . then leap to life, beating as it never had before. Waving, she leaned across the front seat and pushed the door open, but he ran around to her side, dropped his bag, opened the door, reached in, and lifted her out and into his arms.

She clung to him, tilting her head back to meet his kisses. His mouth pressed hungrily against her lips, her cheeks, her eyelids, then hurried back to her mouth. His hands closed around her shoulders, lifting her against him until she stood on tiptoe, clinging to his mouth. The rest of the world vanished. Surrendering herself to the sweet rapture of their kiss, she drew her hands over his neck, shoulders, back, feeling his shirt, damp with sweat, plastered against his hard muscles and warm flesh.

They finally tore themselves apart and stared at each other with a mixture of desire and surprise.

"Oh, baby, that was worth coming two thousand miles!"

"Two million, it was so *wonderful!*" She gasped.

And then they were both laughing, holding tightly for a moment and then letting go of each other and leaning back side by side against the car's hot metal surface, unaware of any heat but what they had generated.

"It was, wasn't it?" Jack chuckled, his eyes traveling slowly over her face. "Well, that makes for a bit of a problem."

Abby cut a glance at him and nodded. "I know what you mean, Gallagher."

Jack laughed. "You do, huh? Think you can read my mind?"

"Uh-huh. It would have been a whole lot simpler if you'd gotten off that plane, kissed me, and we'd both wondered, 'Now, what was all that fuss about?' "

Slipping one hand beneath her hair, he leaned over and tipped her face up to his. "But it didn't happen that way, did it? My heart went bang! Just like last time, and so did yours. You can't hide it. . . . No, don't turn away, Abby. Tell me!"

With an impish grin, she lifted her wide blue eyes to his. "Bang," she whispered.

"I knew it! Call it what you want: Fate, destiny—"

"Temporary insanity?" she offered. "Gallagher, this is crazy. You shouldn't be here. You're not *supposed* to be here. And"—she glanced quickly at her watch —"oh, lordy, neither am I! Oh, Jack, I'm going to be late for everything!"

"Well, just forget I'm here," he insisted, tossing his suitcase in the back seat of Abby's beat-up Dodge station wagon.

Abby stood stock-still, her lips parted in futile protest, and then she rolled her eyes and slid in the front.

Jack climbed inside, making the car seem immeasurably smaller. He leaned back against the door and folded his hands behind his head. "Ready! I'm yours."

She drove north, hurrying to beat the start of rush-hour traffic. As she drove she sneaked eager glances at Jack, and always found him looking at her.

"Have you been here before?"

"No."

"Then pay attention to the scenery, Gallagher. This is central Florida. Disney World is a way to the south behind us."

"I thought that airport was Disney World! A monorail, Mickey and Minnie in every window, parrots in the terminal. Is all of Orlando like that?"

"No. But it *is* big and bustling. Skyscrapers downtown, suburbs sprawling all over. But up where *I* live, there are just small, friendly towns, acres of orange groves, beautiful horse farms, and over a thousand named lakes."

"Thank you, Ms. Chamber of Commerce." Jack grinned.

Abby laughed. "I can't help it. I don't think there's anywhere as pretty."

"I've got my doubts, darlin', but I'm open to persuasion."

There was something in his tone that made Abby's heart skip a beat. She shot him a sideways glance. "Jack, I work. Almost every day. All day long."

"Surely you can find some time for a visiting friend."

The thought, the madness of it, sent shivers up her spine. Looking to change the subject, she asked, "So, where are you staying?"

"With you," he answered coolly.

She took her foot off the accelerator. "You're *what*?" she asked with a gasp as the car lost speed. "Oh, no, you're not! I live in a small town. In an even smaller trailer park. Everyone knows me, and everyone knows I live alone."

"Tell them I'm your cousin—your uncle—your nephew."

"You're crazy! My whole family comes from Hooper, Florida. That's a stone's throw away—twenty minutes northwest, with a population of two-hundred-seventeen. On good days. If a tornado hasn't come through and blown anyone away, or a mad 'gator trotted through and gobbled anyone up. Cousins, uncles, and nephews are known by name, sight, and the kind of breakfast cereal they eat."

"Think you could pick this up over twenty-five, darlin'? That semi's about to roll over us."

"Oops!" she yelped, glancing in her rearview mirror. "See what you do to me? Now, let's be sensible. What I'm going to do is turn this car around and take you back to Disney World. Then I won't feel guilty. You'll have fun; you can go to Fantasyland—"

"My fantasy's right here, Abby Clarke," Jack whispered. He slid one hand down the length of her thigh and let it rest on her knee.

She brushed it off with a despairing flap of her hand. "Don't you dare start anything now, Jack Gallagher. I have got to get back to work. A thousand—no, a *million*—things are waiting, and you are making it impossible to think straight."

She took the first turnaround on the highway and zipped back into the steady flow of cars heading south. Drumming her fingers on the steering wheel, she kept an eye on the traffic around her, frowning into the bright afternoon light. "Okay, first you find a place to stay. And then, if you're still in town, and still interested, I'll see you Monday afternoon."

"But you're the boss—"

"I'm a working boss!"

"Listen," he said softly, serious now that he saw she was. He started to touch her again, but resisted and left his hand on the back of the seat. "Listen, don't send me so far away," he said. "I can't stay long. The season's going to pick up pretty soon, but I've got a break now. Bear's running the rafting outfit alone. I hired a couple of college students for the lodge, but I can't stay away indefinitely because of Pop. I've only got some time—two or three weeks or so. Let's not waste it."

Common sense deserted her. She felt her resolve melt like butter in the sun.

"Jack—"

"I'll behave. I'll stay out of your way during the day. I'll find a river or two—something to keep me busy."

"Promise?"

"Promise," he swore.

Luckily for him, Abby couldn't see into the depths of his gray eyes. After a moment's hesitation, she turned the car around a final time and headed north to Mount Dora and the Paradise Café.

For a restaurant that was still closed for remodeling, it sure was busy! Mrs. LaRue and her cochairman of the garden club, Flo Hopcik, were sitting inside Flo's air-conditioned Cadillac. The seafood distributor was there, water dripping from around the ice-filled crates in the back of his pickup. He was leaning against the cab of the truck, smoking a cigarette and talking to the linen-supply salesman, whose van was parked alongside his. Betty Hogan, from the Chamber of Commerce, was sitting in the shade on the porch swing with Candy Milsap of the Economic Development Council, admiring Abby's geraniums and the new paint job and shutters on the café.

"Gallagher, I could just murder you!" Abby choked out, panic-stricken. She swung the car into the parking lot and jumped out. "Take the car. Find a room. Call me tomorrow," she hissed through the window, then turned around with an apologetic smile. "Hi, everyone. So sorry I've kept you all waiting—"

"No problem, sugar," Candy drawled, speaking for them all. "Boy, the place does look good. I like what you did with the window boxes. . . ." But her glance was focused on the stranger in Abby's car.

Flo and Betty emerged from the Cadillac, bringing streams of cool air with them. "Hurry and open that door, Abby Clarke, before we wilt!" Flo said, laughing, but both women slowed just enough to peek at Abby's unintroduced passenger.

Abby ushered them all in, forbidding herself to look back even once at the parking lot. In moments she was pouring her famous limeades for them all. "Anyone mind if I write up a quick order with Harry first, before his grouper bakes?" She led him into the kitchen and let the door fall shut.

As it did, another opened and Jack Gallagher stepped through the front door into the Paradise Café. The chitchat stopped. Everyone stared. It wasn't often they saw anyone quite like Jack in Mount Dora. It was if a hunk of mountain had tumbled into the Everglades. Standing there, he seemed to fill the doorway, his shirt plastered to the hard, broad muscles of his shoulders and chest, the planes and angles of his handsome face glistening with sweat. It made the women wonder if he was, perhaps, dangerous. The linen-supply salesman would have bet money on it.

Jack stood for a moment, looking around, as much at the place, Abby's place, as at the people. Then, satisfied, he gave an easy smile and walked in.

"We—ah, um—the café's not open for business yet, sir," Candy said, trying to keep her mind on her words while the rest of her memorized that smile.

"I know," Jack answered, pulling a chair away from the nearest table. "I was just hoping for a glass of ice water."

"Let me get you one!" Flo said, leaping to her feet. The women all looked at each other, slightly dismayed but enjoying themselves. Not that much happened in Mount Dora.

"Thank you," Jack said as Flo handed him the frosted glass. He swallowed the contents. "Quite a scorcher, isn't it?"

Edy LaRue lifted one brow. "This is only the end of May. You should see July. But then, you must not be from around here—"

"No."

When he paused they all held their breath, curious but too small-town well-bred to ask.

"I just flew in from Colorado. I'm a friend of Abby's. The name's Jack Gallagher."

They were all in the midst of introductions and handshakes when Abby opened the kitchen door.

"Jack!" She swallowed her surprise, put on her best face, and joined the group. "Well, I'm glad you've gotten to know some of my friends. I would have invited you in for introductions, but I thought you were in a hurry to—uh, to check in to your motel!"

"I am," he replied, grinning, holding her eyes with his brash gaze. "But you rushed off so fast you didn't tell me where to go."

Abby tipped her chin up, matching his grin. "I'd *love* to tell you where to go, Mr. Gallagher—but it might be easier if I just showed you on a map. There's one in the glove compartment."

She led the way back out to the parking lot. The asphalt surface was shimmering in the heat, and the air was thick as soup. Tiny beads of perspiration jumped out along Abby's brow. "Whew! I can't wait for the rainy season to start. Midafternoon the clouds will pile up along the horizon and just sweep in over us, full of thunder and lightning, and it cools everything off."

"Sounds good to me, darlin'! You didn't warn me about this heat."

She jumped down his throat. "There was no reason to warn you, since I never expected to see you again!"

With an intimate touch, Jack brushed the sweat from her forehead. "Now, that would have been a crime, Abby."

Her heart leaped to her throat. Quickly she pressed her fingertips there, as if to hide her far-too-obvious reaction. "Jack, please go. I've got to get back inside."

"I know. I'm going. Can I see you later?"

"I don't know. If I get done early, I was supposed to go to my folks', but you'll have my car. . . ." Her eyes glazed over with confusion, and sharp little lines appeared between her brows. "And now I'm way behind schedule—"

He caught hold of her wrist, a light, loose grip that nonetheless held her captive. "Easy, Abby, easy," he whispered, turning to put himself between her and the café. "I didn't come here to cause you any pain. If you want me to leave, if you really want me to go back to Colorado and make everything simpler, just say so now and I'll be on my way."

Her lips parted. She looked at his face, deep into his slate-gray eyes. Her own eyes darkened with desire. "No, that's not what I want," she whispered.

A smile curved his lips. "Okay, darlin', see you later."

"Tomorrow."

"Sure. Whatever you say." He got in the car and drove away, and Abby went back to work.

Five

At midnight Abby turned the stove off and locked the back door. She called a cab and dropped into a chair, her knees wobbly as Jell-o. She had perfected her sauce, tested the whole opening-night menu, appetizers to desserts, and prepared four dozen puff-pastry shells. Now the last thing she wanted to think about was food! What she *did* want was . . . Well, better not to think of what it was she wanted.

The minute the cab lights swung into the parking lot, she stepped out the front door and locked it, then turned around. "Oh!" she gasped, her breath catching in her throat. Happiness swam into view like a golden fish emerging from murky waters.

Her car was parked there in the center of the lot, a dark shadow waiting behind the wheel.

Already running toward the car, she waved the cab away. "Sorry! My mistake."

"But, lady—"

"It's okay. Go on!"

Abby ran the last few steps to the car and peeked in. Jack was asleep behind the wheel, his head fallen back against the seat. The streetlamp lit a wedge of dark hair, the angle of his jaw. He was so handsome, it took her breath away, and without thinking she reached out and touched his cheek lightly with her fingertips.

"What?" He jumped, banging his head against the roof and jamming his knees against the steering wheel. "Ow! Damn, woman, can't you give a man some warning?" he asked with a growl, rubbing his head.

"Sorry." She laughed, too happy to be truly contrite. "What are you doing here? Why aren't you asleep in some motel or watching HBO on cable TV?"

He glanced balefully in her direction, and then she saw the cut across his forehead, the blood caked on his brow, the already purpling bruise across his cheek. Her throat tightened with fear. "Oh, Lord, what happened to you?"

"I'm fine," he assured quickly, reaching through the open window to take her hand. He flashed her a wry grin. "Honest, I'm fine! Hop in here and I'll explain all about my first day in Florida."

"I don't think I'm ready for this—"

"That's all right. Neither was I." His grin widened, his brashness gleaming as brightly as his teeth.

"Gallagher, you slide over. I'll drive."

"Yes, ma'am." He chuckled, shifting his muscular body out from behind the wheel and farther along the front seat. But not too far. When Abby sat down, the warm, hard length of his thigh pressed against hers. The closeness made her suddenly shy. "So, what happened?" she asked, concerned. "I thought you were looking for a room."

"I found a river."

"Jack!"

"I *was* looking for a room, heading north on 441, scouting out the territory, eyes peeled for a likely motel, and there was this lake, Lake Eustis, lying flat and deep. Not a ripple on it. And these long-legged birds were high-stepping along the shore, right there off the highway—"

"Herons," she said with a sigh, and pulled the car onto the road.

"I know. I asked. Stopped to ask some fishermen about the lake—fishing—rivers, and the next thing I knew, a fellow and I were in his canoe heading down the Dora Canal. Abby"—he grinned in the darkness—"it was damn beautiful. The trees were thick and dark, hanging low over the river—"

"Live oaks—"

"I know. I asked," he said teasingly. "And the branches were hung with moss, like in some Tarzan movie, with the heat shimmering over the surface of the water. Anyway . . ." He slid her a mischievous glance.

"Anyway?" she prompted.

"I saw an alligator. Got so damn excited I stood up for a better look and got whacked in the head with a branch. Knocked me clear out of the canoe."

"Jack! Oh, heavens to Betsy, you really could have gotten hurt. And if it was a 'gator, he could have taken a hell of a bite out of you!"

"Oh, it was a 'gator, all right. I scared the heck out of him: Saw a hundred ninety-five pounds of river rafter heading his way and he gave one good swing of that tail of his and took off."

Laughing, he let his head fall back against the seat. Then he reached over and wound his fingers into her hair. "Hey, I don't want you worrying about me all the time. I get out of more trouble than I get into."

"Just an old habit of mine. Hard to break."

"I'll help," he whispered, slipping his fingers beneath her collar. "So . . . you think you can put me up for the night?"

"Do I have any choice?" she asked, turning the car onto the gravel road that led to her trailer park. But in the dark she was smiling.

They bounced over the loose gravel, passing ghostly

rows of trailers; low, narrow rectangles lined up one after the other. Abby made a sharp left and pulled to a stop below an angled aluminum awning that jutted like the worn brim of a cap from the nearest trailer. "Here we are, Gallagher," she said, half out of the car already. "Come on in and meet Boots and Rascal. But be quiet."

"Do Boots and Rascal like quiet?" he asked jokingly, unfolding himself stiffly from the cramped front seat. Grimacing, he rubbed a kink out of his back, then bent and rubbed his left knee.

"My *neighbors* like quiet," Abby hissed out. "But they like gossip even more, and I want to give them as little excuse as possible." She unlocked the door, snapped on the light, and waved him in. "Hurry up, Jack! Come on."

Inside, he stopped in the middle of the narrow living room, reached up, and touched the ceiling. "Nice place," he said, looking around.

It suddenly seemed a lot smaller than it had when she'd left that morning. "Thanks." She sighed as she saw it all through Jack's eyes. But with a toss of her head she added, "You wouldn't believe what a bargain this was! It belonged to some fisherman, and one day he just took off on a shrimp boat for the Caribbean. I'd been living in one room over the drugstore, and a friend called and said this was available *cheap*. Well, y'all can bet I *raced* over. And I got the trailer and everything he left behind: a frying pan, a pair of jeans, and a great collection of hand-tied flies. I've still got the flies."

"Sounds like the deal of a lifetime." He looked at her with a mixture of humor and admiration. What a little winsome particle of energy she was.

With one broad hand he scooped her up, pulling her close against him, feeling the soft yielding of her breasts against his chest. He bent his head to kiss her and she lifted her face to his, holding her breath, letting her lashes flutter to her cheeks. His mouth was warm and sweet, moving with a firm, hungry pressure over her lips, parting them to let his tongue slip through. Playfully she nipped at the tip of his tongue, then curled her own sensually around his, reckless, and astonished by his nearness. Nothing had ever been so exciting. She felt her tiredness wash away.

Just then a yowling and howling broke the silence. Jack spun, expecting a mountain lion but finding instead two small, fat cats who immediately slipped into the space he had vacated and became busy wrapping themselves around Abby's feet.

"Boots and Rascal," she said apologetically, laughing. "They hate to be ignored."

"Great! I'll remember that."

"Okay, guys, I'm home. Yes, yes, I love you too. Now, let me feed you, and then we'll have our introductions. Jack?" She lifted those great cornflower-blue eyes to his face as she opened a can of cat food. "Are you hungry? Can I get you something?"

"I grabbed some barbecue earlier. I'm fine."

"Coffee?"

"Sounds great."

He watched her move around the tiny space that passed for a kitchen, hypnotized by her quick, neat gestures, her serious, lovely face. She poured fresh black coffee into a pottery mug and set it on the counter in front of him.

"I think I love you, Abby Clarke," he said softly, resting his chin on the palm of one hand.

Abby blushed crimson, the breath stolen from her chest as though some huge hand had just reached in and given her a fierce squeeze. But she cocked her hands on her hips, shook her blond, curly head, and gave him a wry grin. "A mere 'Thanks for the coffee' would be sufficient, Gallagher," she said. "I think that bump on the head was worse than you thought."

He watched her silently, his handsome face unreadable but for the small, sure smile on his lips.

"Cut that out, Gallagher!" she yelped finally. "I'm going to get you something for that cut and then we're—I mean, you and I, separate but equal, are going to bed—I mean, to sleep. Understand?"

He didn't say a word, just sipped his coffee, probably the best cup of coffee he'd ever drunk, and watched her, having probably the best time he'd ever had, sitting in the old, tiny trailer in the middle of the night.

She felt his gaze like a touch on her cheek, her throat, her breasts, the small of her back. "Sit there a minute," she ordered, and vanished into the bathroom. She came back with peroxide, iodine, Band-Aids, a washcloth. "Do you want to do this or should I?" she asked gruffly.

"I'm at your mercy, darlin'."

Standing between his knees, she cleaned the cut on his forehead, painted it with iodine, and patched him up with Band-Aids. Then she rested her hands on his shoulders and kissed the top of his head. "There. I think you'll live."

"Thanks," he said, and reached up to wrap her in his arms.

Dizzy with excitement and plain old exhaustion, Abby slipped away. "Oh, nononono . . ." she warned with a shaky little laugh.

Quickly she pulled sheets and a blanket out of the linen closet and handed them to him. She pointed at the couch. "Good night, Jack," she whispered. "See you in the morning."

She vanished into her room and shut the door.

Minutes later he was knocking at the bedroom door.

"What do you want, Gallagher?" she asked with a groan, jumping into her nightgown.

He walked in and stood grinning at her through the darkness. "Half of me hangs over that couch, and there's not room even on the floor to stretch out. I'd have to carry your furniture into the yard, and then the neighbors would surely wonder. Besides, it's not fair, woman. I comforted you when you were hurt. Seems like you could do the same for me."

She eyed him warily, desire fighting with the last remaining shreds of her sanity. "But then I *knew* nothing would happen."

"How did you know that?"

"I—I trusted you."

"And you can trust me now. Besides, you've been working for sixteen hours straight, and I flew two thousand miles, got hit on the head, and fell in the river on an alligator. You're safe with me tonight. Trust me."

"Gallagher!"

"Abby . . ."

"Okay, but behave." She slipped into one side of the bed and pulled the covers up to her chin. In the dark, he stepped out of his jeans and shirt, slipped in beside her, edged closer.

"Stay on your side, mister!"

"Yes, ma'am."

She reached up to the night table, fumbling in the dark.

"What are you looking for, a gun?"

"No." She laughed. "The alarm."

"Forget it. I'm always up at dawn. Just tell me what time you want to get up."

"Seven. What luxury! But do *not* let me oversleep; I've got to go to my parents' for breakfast. Jack . . . ?"

"Stop worrying. Go to sleep. I'll take care of everything."

"That's what I'm afraid of." She yawned, weary from her long day.

Jack moved closer, circled her narrow waist with his arm, and drew a deep breath, filling his head and lungs with the sweet, delicate scent of her. And like a kitten drawn to the warmth, she snuggled back against him and fell sound asleep.

Later, near dawn, she woke and heard him prowling around outside. With a slap of bare feet on linoleum, she was up and out the door.

A small, wavering greenish light swung back and forth across the path behind the neat row of trailers.

"Jack?"

The flashlight halted mid-swing. "Abby? Hey, I didn't mean to wake you."

"It's okay. Oh, it's beautiful out, isn't it?"

"Hot," came his answer as he stepped into sight, barefoot and bare-chested, wearing only his jeans. He gave her a small, rueful smile. "Guess this wasn't as easy as I thought."

"Nothing is!" Abby laughed. She sank down on the trailer step and wrapped her arms around her knees. "But look at that sky—and that moon—and just listen to those frogs. Brrr-up, brrr-up," she called softly toward the lake.

Jack dropped onto the step next to her. "So, do you often sit in the dark making funny noises?" he asked softly, teasingly, tracing the outline of her cheek with his strong, blunt fingers.

"Never," she answered, catching his hand between her cheek and her bare shoulder. Her eyes shone like stars. "No one's ever tempted me out into the night before."

"Oh, you do know the right thing to say," he whispered, kissing the curve of her neck.

"Never have before," she admitted innocently, and then she took his dark, thick hair in her hands and pulled his face up to hers.

Their mouths met and clung. She filled her soul with his breath and felt suddenly lighter than air. She was floating, flying, dreaming. "I *must* be dreaming," she said against his lips, but he nipped the words away with sharp, stinging love bites. His mouth moved down to her throat and then down to the edge of her nightgown, his tongue rasping hot and wet across the rise of her breast.

Helpless, burning, Abby let her head fall back. Throaty giggles escaped her lips. And then a light flicked on in the trailer next door.

Smothering her laughter behind one hand, she scooted away to the edge of the step. "Whew! That was a close call. The neighbors would have had plenty to talk about."

"So what?" Jack asked with a growl, his eyes narrowed, his chest heaving. Desire had him by the throat. "Why do you worry about that?"

"Because—because . . ." She shrugged, unable to explain something that seemed so obvious. "Because they *are* my neighbors. They know my family: My father and mother, my sister. They know where I come from, and how far I've gotten. And they admire me for that."

"What does that have to do with anything, Abby?"

How do I answer that? she wondered. Why, she'd never even really thought about it before. It was just part of her life, part of who she was. All those years of work, all the struggle and the hard climb up from nothing had earned her their respect, their admiration. That was *not* something to be treated lightly. That was *not* something to be risked. But how could she explain it to someone as self-confident as Jack?

The silence stretched between them, still and heavy as the humid southern night.

Jack reached out and tipped her chin up. "Sorry, Abby. I didn't mean to push."

"You weren't." She wished for the first time in her life that she were the kind of person who could open up, speak her heart. But she wasn't. Instead she said softly, "You just take some getting used to." Then she laughed out loud. "And boy, oh, boy, are you going to take some explaining in Hooper!"

Daylight sneaked up on them, painting the box-like shapes of the trailers a crisp, clean white. There were round little hedges at each door, mowed lawns, striped awnings, and beach chairs. Bicycles rested against porches, baseball bats lay on the grass. The lake looked like a blue circle of silk, and cabbage palms waved their tall, spiky heads around the shore. A great blue heron lifted its hinged legs in a slow, stately dance that made circles appear on the surface of the lake, then thrust its beak into the water and came up with a fish.

"Hungry?" Abby asked, tilting her face up to look at Jack.

"Getting there," he agreed.

"Good, because at my folks', breakfast hits the table at sunup. Ready?"

"This is home," Abby said, waving a hand out the driver's window as they neared town an hour later. "Small, quiet. When I was growing up there were twelve houses in town. Dirt roads. And those dead orange trees were all so green, you would have thought someone had polished each leaf by hand. And heavy with fruit. Oh, it was pretty! There were groves all around us, as far as I could see. My father managed a grove for a wealthy owner who lived up near Jacksonville, and though we didn't own a stick, it gave us a certain amount of prestige." Her eyes twinkled with mischief. "In fact, our house was the first one in town with a flush toilet! I charged every neighborhood kid a penny to come flush it!"

"An entrepreneur even then!" He laughed, unreasonably happy at the sight of her smile.

"You bet! I knew money was the key."

There was a small silence. "To what?"

"To everything I didn't have. Everything my parents didn't have. To security, and knowing you had your house and a meal on the table, and braces for your kid sister—"

"What about you?" Jack asked, burying his hand up to the wrist in her blond hair.

Abby smiled. "Someone up there must have known we couldn't afford it yet, and blessed me with good, straight white teeth."

"And that cute nose, and those heavenly blue eyes, and a ripe, luscious mouth—"

"Gallagher"—Abby groaned—"don't you be giving me a bad time now at my folks'."

"That's your trouble, darlin'! You don't know a good time from a bad time." He dipped his fingers beneath the collar of her blouse.

Abby swatted his hand away. "I was telling you about Hooper. There's the church. The drive-in bank. Our one and only grocery store. The drugstore used to have a real soda fountain, and you could get lemon Cokes that burned your throat and brought you back to life on a hot summer afternoon. And there's Mr. Lucas—Hi, Ernie!" she yelled, waving. "How's Phoebe?" Then, to Jack: "That's his collie. She needed surgery last week."

Assured that all was well, she turned the corner at the gas station and called to a woman pumping gas into an old Mercury. "Hi, Ruthie! We open Friday. Y'all come by!" Still waving, she slowed, put on her blinker, and pulled into a narrow driveway lined with palmettos and a few drooping petunias. "Poor things need rain," she muttered, and jumped from the car. "Coming?"

"Whither thou goest, I will go . . ." he quoted, catching her so by surprise, she tripped over her own feet. Jack threw back his head and laughed. "Haven't spent all my life on the river, darlin'. Lead on."

Abby's blood was percolating like coffee on high. Flushed, weak-kneed, her palms clammy, she led the way around to the kitchen door.

They were almost there when a girl tumbled out, wearing a bikini top and shorts so short, they gave new meaning to the word. "Fi-nally!" she shouted, then froze, staring wide-eyed at Jack. "Hoo-eee. *Who* are *you?*"

Abby groaned, shutting her eyes. "Jeanette . . ."

"What *is* the commotion?" her mother's call interrupted from inside.

"Oh, this is going to be fun!" Jeanette giggled and held the door open. "Mom, Dad. Abby's here. And she has brought us some company."

Taking Jack into that tiny, crowded kitchen was like introducing a lion to a herd of deer grazing at a water hole. Her folks were small people, lean and burned dark by the sun. She could see their surprise, dismay, nervousness. She talked quickly, hoping to calm them, telling them that she'd met Jack in Colorado, but not how. With a lift of her brows, she asked for his help.

Jack followed her lead, shaking hands all around, talking soft and easy about his life out west, his mountains, the High Pines Lodge. Her folks began to relax.

Seated at the breakfast table, Jeanette kept the conversation going a hundred miles an hour. "Do you ski out there? I water-ski. My friend Tige, he's just a friend-boy, and not a boyfriend, he's got a ski boat on Lake Griffin, and I'm learning to jump slalom. Did Abby tell you she can ski barefoot? Honest! And she can surf. And—"

"Jeanette, hush! Jack doesn't want to hear all this."

"Sure, I do," Jack said with a wink.

"Good. We don't want him to think all you can do is cook! Well, she was voted most likely to succeed by her high-school class. Me, I was voted prom queen."

"I would have preferred a scholarship to FSU." Abby sighed.

"Amen to that." Her mother nodded, but gave her younger daughter a loving look.

"We each march to a different drummer," Jeanette chirped on happily.

"My day for surprise quotes!" Abby laughed, amazed, then waved away their questioning looks. "More grits, Jack? Ham?"

Jack pushed himself away from the table. "Couldn't eat another bite, but it was great. Thank you."

Abby's father rose from his seat. "How about if we take our coffee out on the porch? I've got a red-cockaded woodpecker I've been keeping an eye out for in those pines."

Her father led the way, settling in an old wooden rocker and pointing Jack into another. He picked up his binoculars, scanned the trees, and then dropped his hands in his lap. He sat in silence as the moments ticked by. When Abby and her mother brought the coffee out in heavy pottery mugs, he blew across the surface of his, watching the steam lift and waiting for everyone to settle down. Then he looked off into the trees again.

"So, you like my girl, do ya?" her father asked in a tone that indicated he was unused to such conversation.

"Dad!" Abby gasped, open-mouthed with shock.

But her father was determined to have his say. He met Jack's calm look with a nod, stretched out his stiff legs, and nodded again. "Yup, thought so. Well, has she told you much about herself? Nope, thought not. That's the way she is. But I'll tell you, that's some special girl there. Without her, we'd be living in a one-room shack in the middle of scrub oaks, and not this purty place. Me, I put my trust in the groves and the weather, and both failed me. Nothin' to show for a life's work, and nowhere to turn. But Abby, she stepped in. She done things I never could do."

"Dad, don't—" Abby said, laying a hand on his arm and desperately avoiding Jack's gaze.

"I'm not sayin' anything out of place, daughter. Just want this fella to know what kind of girl you are. See, she doesn't bring many fellas around, so I thought this was worth sayin'. Now, how about some more coffee?"

"Thank you," Jack answered evenly, just the hint of a smile tugging at his mouth.

"I'll get it!" Abby jumped up. Her cheeks were blazing.

"I think you just got it!" Jeanette burst out laughing. "Oh, it's great to have someone else in the hot seat, for a change. Especially my big sister!"

Abby fled into the kitchen.

Jack tracked her inside. He stopped in the doorway and leaned one shoulder against the wall, letting his eyes play lovingly over her slender frame. "Abby, please don't be embarrassed."

She spun around, looking wide-eyed and flushed. "Oh, but I am! That was awful! How could they? How could my father? He's usually so quiet, so reserved." Squeezing her eyes shut, she gave a little shudder at the memory.

"Then it must be my fault," Jack said, grinning. "He must have seen the wild look I get in my eyes when you're near me."

There was a second of silence, and then Abby laughed. "Okay, Jack, yes, I'll blame it on you. Just please, don't you pay attention to everything everyone says. Oh, family! And Jeanette! Sometimes I think she's going to be the death of me."

"I think she's cute. And stop worrying, she'll grow up. Don't you remember raising hell when you were a kid?"

"No," Abby said honestly, and turned to get the coffee pot.

Jack crossed the kitchen and reached around her waist, holding the counter edge with both hands, trapping her in the circle of his arms. "Then it's a good thing I showed up when I did."

Abby felt the floor give way again. Yes. Yes, how nice to stop being the responsible, serious adult for a moment. To flirt with this beautiful man, laugh with him, touch him. How nice to relax and be silly with him, sexy with him. Her blue eyes shone. "Maybe it is, Mr. Gallagher."

Six

But Abby forgot all about having fun in the days that followed.

With less than a week until her grand opening, she was frantic. She ran from one place to another, and at first she thought someone had dropped a ponderosa pine smack dab in the middle of her path.

"Jack, why don't you go canoeing or sailing—or *something?*" she'd ask.

"Then I'd be too far away to do this—" He would laugh and trap her in his arms, rubbing her soft cheek with the first shadow of his beard.

"Stop! Let go! I have got to order the catfish. And hire another busboy. And check that the ads are running—"

And Jack would lower his dark head and stop her protests with the firm, demanding pressure of his mouth. He'd nip the words right off her lips, making her head spin, her heart flutter.

"Jack," she'd whisper then, "please go paddle a river, or tickle an alligator. My tomatoes are spoiling, my ice is melting, my tablecloths are getting permanent creases!"

"All right." He would give that irresistible grin of

his, the grin that melted her from the inside out and left her trembling and breathless. "All right, but I'll be back by dark. And then I'm taking you to dinner. No argument, lady."

Tuesday morning Jeanette came by, a sweat shirt flapping against her bare thighs, her bikini invisible beneath its voluminous folds. "Come on, Jack, I'm going to teach you to water-ski!"

He left laughing and came back laughing, but bruised and sore and stiff. "Whew! That was one helluva workout! Makes me think I'm gettin' old, baby." He smiled at Abby.

"No one told you to try to *jump* first time out!" Jeanette scolded, but her eyes shone with adoration. "*No one* jumps the first time out, Jack! And, Abby," she said, giggling, "you should have just seen Tige. He thinks Jack's the greatest. Followed him around like a puppy, trying to walk like him, talk like him, he even—oops, here he comes, don't let him know I was tellin' on him."

"Can I come in, Ms. Clarke?" the boy called nervously through the screen.

"Great! You're Superman and I'm the Wicked Witch of the South," she whispered with mock ferocity to Jack. "Yes, Tige. Come right in. I don't bite, you know."

The boy entered, blushing. "I just didn't want to be in the way."

"In the way? Of what? No one's letting me get a lick of work done, anyway," she said, scowling.

Jeanette gave her a quick hug. "Oh, sis, are you jealous 'cause you had to work while we had such a great time?"

"Great time! Two of you look like you've caught a terminal case of hero worship, and one of you looks like he got run over by a Mack truck. No. I'm glad I stayed here and accomplished something."

"Uh-oh, she's jealous, all right. That's the same

in her. It was a longing as strong as hunger or thirst. It flickered to life deep inside and burned outward along every nerve. *Is this enough? Is this all I want?* No! her heart insisted with every beat. No! And suddenly she couldn't stand still, couldn't concentrate on the lovely, firm fish, the pale-peach-colored sauce, and the plump avocados. . . .

The whole room spun. Grabbing the edge of the counter, she fanned her face with a towel. "Get hold of yourself, girl! Remember who you are and all the people counting on you!"

Stubbornly she straightened her shoulders and tightened her apron strings. Grabbing a knife, she quickly reduced a mango to a fan of sweet, pale-orange slices.

"What in the world are you doing, Abby?" Simon asked as the kitchen door swung shut behind him. "You're supposed to be out there looking stunning in that little green dress of yours and mingling with the guests."

"I'm supposed to be doing exactly what I *am* doing, Simon. It's what I do best!" she insisted, trying not to be annoyed with him that night. "You go on and mingle. Just let me know how everything goes out there."

"Need you ask? It's fantastic. Absolutely fantastic. By the way, I think we could save a bundle by setting out brown-'n'-serve rolls instead of those piña-colada muffins of yours."

"I don't *serve* frozen rolls, Simon."

"Well, other than that, dear one, everything is just wonderful." He smoothed his tux and smiled at his reflection in the oven window. "And now I'd better get back to greeting our customers."

He pushed open the door to the dining room, but then popped his head back in. "Hey, your family's here."

A rush of happiness filled her heart. Whipping off her apron, she hurried past him.

Her parents stood there in the doorway, side by side, dressed in their very best, beaming with pride and happiness. Above the knot of his unaccustomed tie, her father's Adam's apple bobbed with emotion. Her mother had tears in her eyes.

At the sight of them, Abby's own eyes filled with tears. She hurried over and hugged them, then reached past them for Jeanette and hugged her too. "I'm so happy you're all here with me!"

Then she stole a glance over Jeanette's shoulder. "Where's Jack?" she whispered. "I thought you were coming together."

"Oh, he's around," Jeanette said, and grinned.

"Maybe he had to go find him a parking spot way up in Leesburg," her father said teasingly. "This little place of yours has brought people from all over!" He gave her hand a quick squeeze. "We sure are proud of you, girl."

"Thank you. Thank you all." She led them to a special table by the window. "This," she said with a flourish, "is our new menu, and I want you to try everything! And Simon's opened lots of champagne, so have a good time, and I'll be back as soon as I can."

She raced back to the kitchen.

Jack was there, making Lena and Archie nervous as all get-out with his presence, and Abby only made it worse when she ran to him and wrapped her arms around his neck.

"What are you doing coming in the back door, stranger?"

"I needed one minute alone with you. Just to congratulate you—and give you these." He pulled a dozen long-stemmed yellow roses out from behind his back. "Success and happiness, Abby," he whispered, filling her arms with flowers. "I love you."

Abby pulled him into the pantry.

"Hush, Jack. Not in front of my help!" she whispered. But, lifting herself on tiptoe, she kissed him full on the mouth.

Laughing, he gazed at her with tender exasperation. "How typically Abby! I know it's a four-letter word, darlin', but I don't think they'll be too shocked —or are you just afraid they'll know you're human, and want this as much as I do?" And he kissed her right back, long and hard enough to make her knees buckle.

A sudden sharp knock on the pantry door made them both jump. "Ms. Clarke, you in there? There's orders comin' in. You want me to do the cookin' for a while?"

She yelped. "No, of course not, Lena!" She spun and brushed a hasty kiss across Jack's lips. "Thank you for the flowers, Jack, and for bringing my family, and—"

"Go cook!" He laughed.

"Later," she swore as she hurried through the kitchen to put the roses in a vase. "Later we'll have time."

"I know. Later," he repeated as he followed her.

She turned and froze as she saw the flicker of something deep in his dark eyes. Her heart thudded once, twice, against her ribs. "Jack, is everything all right?"

He looked into her hopeful upturned face.

"Yes. Fine," he assured her, and leaned one broad shoulder against the kitchen wall. "I'll just stand here and watch you. I've missed doing that these last few days."

"And I missed you too!" She laughed as she put the roses in a vase.

Simon came in and caught her blushing. His sly glance swung around the kitchen. "Oh, look who's here."

"Hello, Simon."

"Hello, Jack."

The greeting was cold. Although they had crossed paths only a few times during the week, it was obvious the two men didn't like each other, and they didn't waste much effort trying to hide it.

"Archie," Simon ordered, "go get me another case of champagne. I've got it chilling in the walk-in." He swung back to Jack. "So, what do you think of our grand opening?"

"It's great. Congratulations. And I wish you both the best of luck."

"Thanks. You're a prince."

Anyone who knew him better would have cringed at the flash of anger in Jack's dark eyes. But Simon blandly drew two bottles from the case Archie carried in and headed for the door. "Bring the rest, Archie," he commanded, and disappeared.

Abby let her breath out with a hiss. "Ohhh, that partner of mine!"

Jack stared at the closed door, willing the anger out of his face, but his voice still had an edge to it when he muttered, "There's some safety in being stupid."

Then he turned to Abby and drew a finger across her cheek. "Just don't let him spoil your night, Abby. He isn't worth it."

Abby took his advice and reveled in the rest of the evening. As she cooked, she kept up a stream of chatter about the dishes she was preparing, the customers, the town, old local yarns about citrus and railroads and Seminoles—and about her own childhood. She felt as though she had the best of everything: The Paradise open again and Jack there to share it!

All of a sudden it was midnight. The last customer was ushered, full and smiling, out the door. Abby dropped back against it, radiant with happiness.

"We did it! Boy, oh boy, did we ever! Did you hear those compliments? Did you feel that excitement? They loved us!"

"What's not to love?" Jack answered, grinning back at her.

"Damn right!" Simon chimed in. "Here, let's drink to the best partnership south of the Mason-Dixon!" He poured two glasses of champagne, then reluctantly filled a third.

"Oh, let's have *everyone* celebrate!" Abby said, too happy to pay any attention to his pettiness. "Everyone front and center!" she called, and poured glasses of champagne for Lena and Archie and even a tiny bit for her two busboys. "Okay, crew, here's to all of us!"

Cleaning up, they finished off another bottle of champagne. Tipsy, tired, but totally happy now, Abby turned on the radio and did a little two-step around the room.

Jack watched her for a moment, his dark eyes reflecting a slim, pretty girl in an emerald green dress, its thin straps falling off her shoulders, its skirt swinging about her legs—and then he had to hold her. When he took her in his arms, they danced around the tables. He moved lightly for such a big man, country-dancing her around the room, then swinging her into a little lindy. Happy, laughing, they looked deep into each other's eyes.

Simon's jealousy was written plainly on his face. "Well, if you don't need me, I'm going home." His voice was a whine. "I'm exhausted!"

" 'Night," Abby replied, matching her steps to Jack's, swinging out to the beat of the music, catching Jack's hand and sliding back into the warm curve of his arm. Spinning out and back, she felt the world spin with her like a merry-go-round, while she held the golden ring. When a slow song came on, she leaned contentedly against Jack's chest, wrapped her arms around his neck, and closed her eyes.

There was a knock on the door.

"We're closed!" Abby called happily, resting her cheek against Jack's shoulder. "Come back tomorrow for lunch!"

The knocking continued, growing louder and more insistent.

She and Jack shared a quick, puzzled look, and then Abby shrugged out of his arms and opened the door.

Two men, dressed by *Gentleman's Quarterly*, but nasty-looking, leaned against the doorway.

Abby took an involuntary step back. "I'm sorry, we're closed."

"But we were invited to the party," the older, slicker of the two answered with a leer. "We're here to see Simon."

"Simon's left," Jack said, stepping from the shadows. He placed himself between Abby and the door. "You can leave a message."

The two laughed unpleasantly, as if sharing some in joke. They looked casually around Jack's solid bulk at the dining room. "Sure, tell him his partners were here. Tell him we drove all the way from Miami and were sure sorry to miss all the fun."

"I'll tell him."

"Hey, is that the little lady he's in business with?"

Jack stiffened. Abby could almost see the hair rise along the back of his neck. It was like seeing two hyenas taunt a lion. But Jack only shifted his weight, took his hands from his pockets, and stared at them coldly.

"Hey, no problem, man!" The first backed off. "See, we're his partners, and she's *his* partner, and that sort of makes us relatives, don't it? We're just looking to be friendly."

"Nice of you," Jack said.

"Yeah," one said. "We're nice guys."

In tandem they swaggered over to a silver Mercedes and drove away.

"Yuck!" Abby exclaimed, wiping her damp palms on her apron skirt. "That was like a scene from 'Miami Vice.' "

Jack shut the door and turned to her. "What do you know about Simon?"

Abby shrugged. "Not that much. I had my lawyer check him out when he approached me with the partnership offer. He ran a credit check, got references, all of that stuff."

"And what did you learn?"

"He's rich. Family money. He'd made some good investments in real estate down in Coconut Grove and the Keys. He even owns a restaurant, a raw bar, in Key Largo, and it's making money. He sounded good. And he was willing to let me keep control of the operations end."

"Then why the complaints that he's always butting into your ordering, your menus, your kitchen help?"

"Well"—she sidestepped, feeling horribly uncomfortable—"he hasn't quite stuck to that part of the bargain."

"Make him," Jack said shortly.

"Make him?" Abby gasped. "How?" She jutted her chin out at him, her eyes flashing.

"Tell him to stay the hell out of the food end or it's finished."

"Finished?" she echoed, her hands and voice suddenly trembling. "*I'd* be finished! I haven't got a cent without his money, and I'm up to my ears in debt for all this remodeling, and—and I probably shouldn't have done it all, but I've always had this dream, and—and—" Tears spilled down her cheeks.

"Hush, darlin'. Shhh." He grabbed her and held her close, his handsome face twisted in pain. "Hush, don't cry. I'm sorry. Damn me, I didn't mean to make you cry!"

There was a haze of pain in his eyes, and his voice was a strangled groan as he tipped her face up and wiped it with the tips of his fingers.

Some salty tears escaped his hands and raced to the corners of her mouth. She swiped at them with the tip of her tongue. "Now, why did I do that?" She laughed in embarrassment. "Oh, goodness, this isn't like me at all!"

Jack's laugh was husky with relief. "Sure! I've heard that before."

"Oh, Gallagher, you do bring out the baby in me." She shook her head in dismay.

"I can love the baby in you as much as I love the woman. Just let me take care of you a little. I've got two strong arms. Let me hold you safe. It would do me good too," he whispered, and wrapped her in his arms.

"Oh, you're sweet, Gallagher."

"No, not sweet. Selfish. I'm running out of time, darlin'. I'm going to have to go back—at least for a while—"

"No!" she cried with sudden, unexpected fierceness. "No, don't say that. I won't let you talk about that tonight!"

"But, Abby—"

"No! It's too unfair. I *had* to work hard this week, and I lost all that time with you, and I will *not* talk about your going back. That's all. That's final."

He stood still, a war raging silently inside him, visible only in the muscles tensing in his jaw.

Abby refused to see. Letting go of the stranglehold she had on him, she raised her hands to his strained face and playfully lifted the corners of his mouth. "Don't look so worried. We'll work it out, Gallagher."

"I know that, dammit!" He groaned. "But it isn't easy."

"Who said anything about easy?" she murmured, leaning her cheek on his shoulder. "But we got through opening night—"

"Had a fabulous opening night!" he corrected, stroking the delicate ridge of her spine.

"Yes, you're right. And tomorrow night will be a breeze. And then I have all Sunday off! Interested?"

"Vaguely," he answered softly. He bent his head and nuzzled against the tender skin of her throat, then caught her earlobe between his teeth and gave it a sharp little nip.

"Jack!" Giggling, she wriggled against him, flooded by the now-familiar stirring of her passion. "Let me turn off the lights, and we'll go home," she whispered.

He leaned back, narrowing his eyes. "We'll go to my place."

"*Your* place?" she echoed. "You mean your motel?"

"I found a houseboat for short term rental on the St. Johns. Docked it at a curve of the river. And I've got a Jeep to get us there."

"Oh, you'll never change." She laughed.

"Do you want me to?" His expression was serious.

"No, not at all."

They locked up the Paradise and stepped out into the heavy, sultry night. "Whew!" Jack muttered, drawing a deep breath. "This is like filling your lungs with wet cotton!"

"It gets better," Abby assured him, slipping her hand into his. "The rain will start soon. Then you'll see something!"

They were quiet as he headed the car out onto the highway. She sat close to him, absorbing the reassuring solidness of his body through her arm, her hip, her thigh. The warm, hard length of him was more soothing than all those glasses of champagne.

"It will all be okay, won't it?" she asked, looking up at him.

"Yes, darlin', it'll be okay. I'll help you make it

okay. I promise." And he dropped an arm around her shoulders.

She rested her cheek against his shoulder, and never felt the rising tide of her exhaustion as it rose up to claim her.

The next thing she knew was that she was being carried somewhere, as lightly and carefully as a baby, and dropped down into the cool, floating peace of sleep.

She woke up early and alone, and looked around in surprise. The sun was streaming in the windows, a thousand frogs were singing, and the bed rocked gently back and forth, back and forth.

And then she realized where she must be, and hurried, dressed only in her sleep-wrinkled slip, through the short hallway of the houseboat.

Jack was sitting at the kitchen table, reading a month-old copy of *Sports Illustrated* and drinking coffee.

" 'Morning," she said softly, and then steadied her footing as the boat rode the wake of a passing motorboat. "This is fun!" She smiled, feeling suddenly shy.

Jack was bare-chested, his jeans slung low on his hips, his bare feet pushed into a pair of sneakers. His hair was rumpled, but his eyes looked as if he hadn't slept in weeks. His gaze lingered hungrily on the silk-covered curves of her breasts and hips, the hollow of her throat, the tousled blond hair.

With great effort he offered her a smile. "Glad you like it, Abby."

"Oh, I do. Okay if I get a cup of coffee?"

"Of course," he answered, his voice low and husky.

She sat across from him at the table. "Funny, but I guess I didn't realize how worn out I was. I fell asleep, huh?" She bit her lower lip. "So—what happened?" She was teasing, trying to be cute.

"Same as always, darlin'. Nothing at all." He was also teasing, but only partly.

This was getting damn hard to deal with, and he could feel the tension rising within him, building, threatening to explode. A few more days like this and there'd be hell to pay. Dammit! And there she sat, all tanned skin and blond hair, that mouth that kept him from wanting any other mouth, those eyes that gave back the only image of himself he wanted.

"Dammit," he cursed, and sent his coffee spilling across the tabletop. "Doesn't it ever rain down here?"

Seven

Saturday was a scorcher. And on Sunday you could have fried an egg on the sidewalk outside the Paradise Café, but neither Abby nor Jack was there to see it happen.

Jack came banging on her screen door at six in the morning, making a racket that woke the dogs to barking all around the trailer park. On the lake behind him, a pair of herons rose up in wing-flapping alarm. And inside Abby's narrow white trailer, Boots hissed in fright and raked twenty needle-thin tracks in the upholstery of her favorite chair.

Abby flew to the door. "Who is it? What do you want?" she yelled, pulling it open the length of the metal chain. "Jack!" She slammed it shut to free it and threw the door wide open. "What the hell are you doing here, Gallagher? It's predawn on my one day off! Are you crazy? I want to be sleeping—"

"You can sleep in the car," he said. Leaping up the steps, he took her in his arms and half-hugged, half-danced her back into the trailer. "Hurry up! Put on some little bathing suit, the skimpier the better. We're going to the beach."

"On Sunday?" She groaned, lingering happily in

his arms. "It'll be mobbed. Why don't we just stay here, lazy around, cook something up—" She grinned, then lifted herself on tiptoe to kiss his mouth.

He kissed her back with playful fervor, but then spun her around and gave her an encouraging push toward the bedroom. "Promises, promises, darlin'. Nope! If we stay here you'll sleep or work, as usual—and I've got other plans!"

How do you argue with a man who won't take no for an answer?

In moments Jack's Jeep was racing toward the still-dark sky over the Gulf Coast. Abby felt the last traces of sleepiness blow away on the warm, damp morning wind that tugged at her hair and flattened the thin cotton of her T-shirt against her breasts. "Life's a Beach" was printed in a carefree scrawl across the front, and of course when she had first put it on over her bikini, Jack had had to trace it oh, so slowly with one fingertip.

"Cut that out!" she had scolded between heated giggles.

"I will not." And before she could say another word, he had grabbed her close, tightened his fingers around a handful of curls, and slipped his tongue between her lips into the sweet, honeyed cave of her mouth.

Remembering, she felt again the swift, powerful surge of arousal that sparked between her legs and spread through every inch of her body. Parts of her she hardly knew existed suddenly tingled and throbbed. If a kiss could do that, then they'd find bits and pieces of her exploded all over the Gulf Coast if this day was headed where she thought—no, hoped!—it was.

"What are you grinning at, woman?" Jack asked, his slate-gray eyes glinting with amusement.

"Nothing." She laughed. "Just wondering where we're headed."

"Clearwater Beach. Okay with you?"

"Fine. Anything's fine."

Jack gave her a cool, swift glance of suspicion.

Such complaisance was unheard-of in Abby Clarke. But she sat there like an angel in the morning, the first rays of the sun lighting the pale cloud of her hair, outlining the narrowness of her shoulders, the perfect curve of her chin and cheek. Her eyes were even bluer than the morning sky, bluer than the rivers he ran, bluer than that lake in the desert.

He tightened both hands on the wheel and prayed he could keep as good a grip on his desire. "Damn," he muttered, battling the urge simply to pull off onto the side of the road, toss her into a pile of palmetto leaves, and love her to death. "Damn!"

"What's the matter?" Abby asked, putting a cool hand on his arm.

"Nothing! Just talk to me for a while."

"Okay." She gave him a funny little look, but shrugged. "Well, the Paradise had a great night last night. We had reservations for all but two tables, and a line—"

"Nope, no talk about work."

A pout and a shrug. "Ooo-kaaay. Well, I talked Jeanette into signing up for *two* classes in summer school, and—"

"Nope, no talk about Jeanette. Or your parents. *Or* your cats, hound dog or partner, in that order."

"Well, that doesn't leave much, Gallagher!"

"It leaves the whole world, Abby."

For a moment she was startled into ornery silence. Then she looked around and smiled. Yes, it did, didn't it! So she told him about the taste of a fresh-picked orange, how warm it was, sweeter than candy as the juice dripped down her chin; and she told how the orange seeds were planted for budwood, and the baby trees would grow straight and tall, and the growers would prune them back to make them bush out, and when they'd bud, you'd cut off the "eyes," or tiny buds, and then graft them onto the root stock, and bingo, you'd have fruit in two years, *unless* there was a freeze, or canker. And when there was canker, the trees were cut down and burned, all those lovely trees, all that work and hope and all those dreams for the future gone. And if you were lucky and there was no canker, *then* you worried about frost; and if a cold front was coming, you got out and started up the tractor and banked the trees and sprayed them with water to protect them with an icy coat. But there were never enough men to run the pumps day and night, because they were on their own groves trying to work the same miracle; and hardly anyone could afford heaters—even the big owners couldn't afford the fuel—and the trees died, and she'd watched her father's frozen hands hang hopeless at his sides, her mother's hands wringing the bottom of her apron in despair. *But if the trees didn't die*—well, there was nothing more beautiful in the whole world!

And as they neared Tampa, she told him how the pirate ships would sail into Tampa Bay every February on Gasparillo Day and "attack" the city.

And when they passed the turnoff to Tarpon Springs she told him about the Greek fishing village, with its fleet of ships and its fabulous food!

And by eight-fifteen they were standing on the beach with their toes in the Gulf of Mexico.

Jack tossed a blanket on the sand, kicked off his sneakers, and pulled his shirt up over his head.

Abby wanted to reach out and rub her hands over that massive chest, those wonderful shoulders, that smooth, broad back. He was so dark now, bronzed by days of fishing and canoeing and skiing, and his body had the look of touchable perfection. She felt her palms itch with desire, matching the general itch that seemed to seize her body, leaving her breathless, dizzy, unnerved.

"You okay?" Jack asked, worry clouding his eyes.

"Fine!" she chirped, shading her eyes with one hand flat as she looked up at him. "I think I'll just sit down for a minute."

"Sun, that's what it is. You haven't been out in the sun in days! And I didn't stop and get you any breakfast. Sorry." He knelt next to her on the blanket, brushing the hair back from her flushed cheeks. "Here." He turned and pawed through the knapsack he had flung down on the sand. "Bagels. Oranges. Granola bars . . ."

Abby took a cinnamon-and-raisin bar and nibbled on it, amused by his misplaced concern, yet sweetly charmed. "I'm fine. Really. What else have you got in there?"

"Two hats. Sunglasses. Suntan oil—"

"Great!" Abby sat up suddenly, stretching a hand out and wiggling her fingers. "I'd better put some on you before you get burned!"

"Me?" He laughed. "You're the one with places pale as moonlight." He shook his head and began to unscrew the cap.

"No! I insist! Just lie down here, and I'll put a little on your back, your shoulders, your chest. . . ." She was already squeezing the oil into the trembling palm of her hand and reaching out to touch him.

Jack lifted his chin, staring at her with a loving, knowing look. "Sounds good to me, darlin'." He stepped out of his jeans and lay facedown on the blanket. Resting his cheek on his folded arms, he smiled to himself as she stroked the warm oil across his skin.

She started at the small of his back, brushing the top of his bathing suit with her fingers, spreading her hands out over the smooth bands of muscle that covered his ribs, and up his spine, circling out again over the broad span of his shoulder blades, her fingers coming together and then sweeping out across his flesh, pushing the muscles that lay just beneath the warm, velvet skin, feeling the muscles resist, then yield to her light, trembling touch.

Turning beneath her hands, he rolled onto his back. A teasing smile masked the husky yearning in his voice. "This side was getting lonesome, darlin'."

Though his lids were narrowed against the bright glare of the sun, Abby could see the sharp glints of desire that surfaced from the depths of his eyes. But he held himself still, crossed his arms beneath his head and looked up at her. "You know, you don't need any excuse to touch me. Wanting to is enough."

Abby shakily rubbed oil across his chest. Her fingers tangled in the mat of dark, curly hair, leaving streaks of oil against his dark, smooth skin. She felt dizzy, giddy, her head spinning from the growing warmth of the sun on her head and shoulders and the steady, burning heat of Jack's body. She felt like a crystal icicle suspended between the two, melting, melting till nothing remained but the fierce blue flame at the heart of her.

Desperate to ease her tension, she forced a high little laugh and rocked back on her heels. "Whooee! There's so much of you, I don't know if I have enough energy to finish this job!"

Jack whooped with laughter. "You little nut!" He pulled her down on top of him, using his arms and legs to pin her against him, locking her there against his pounding heart while he kissed her moist, ready mouth. "I'm sure," he whispered against her lips, "you have enough energy for *this.*"

A high titter of giggles burst from a cluster of palms behind them. "Shh. Look at 'em kissin'!"

Abby squirmed off Jack and jumped to her feet just in time to see a covey of six-year-olds turn tail and flee across the beach. Her face flamed with embarrassment. "I can't believe it!"

"Heck—" Jack was propped on one elbow, grinning at her. "There are worse things they could see, darlin'." He fell back on the sand, but kept watching her as she modestly smoothed her shorts and straightened her shirt with trembling, sandy fingers. "You know something?" he announced. "I love you. No doubt about it."

Abby's heart did a somersault. And then she was

smiling, her face shining with the truth and joy of it. "And I love you, Jack," she said right out loud, and, floating back to his side, she sank down onto the sand, leaned over, and kissed him full on the mouth. "I really do."

"I know, baby, and I'll spend my life making you glad you do."

Suddenly fireworks were bursting in her head, skyrockets of excitement shooting through her veins. She didn't know what to do with herself, with this wild, unexpected delight. Leaping to her feet, she quickly took off the T-shirt and shorts, revealing her tiny bikini, and sped down toward the water's edge. "Come on!" she yelled. "Last one in's a rotten egg!"

They yelled and splashed and swam, gave each other salty kisses, and slipped their hands over each other's slick, sea-cooled skin. For a little while the water hid their arousal, and they jumped and played and pretended they were *only* having fun. Jack's hands at her waist were only there to lift her over a dip in the sea floor. Her yelps and cries were only from the sudden, unseen dart of a fish against her leg. And when she jumped up against his chest, her hands on his shoulders, she was only trying to duck him under the water. But as she floated back down against the water-slick front of his body, he slipped a knee between her legs and she rode there against him, her arms wrapped around his neck, her breasts flattened against his chest, the hard muscular feel of his thigh between her thighs the only reality her mind could comprehend.

She clung to him, the power of her arousal frightening and thrilling in its intensity. She wanted him so badly, it hurt. Almost weeping with frustration, she broke away.

"I—I'm getting out," she stammered. "I need a—a little air."

"We need to love each other, darlin'. That's what we need. Just like the tide's gotta rise, and the sun's gotta shine—"

"Yes! yes, I know it too. And I want to! Right now, right this moment! Quick, let's go find a motel—" And she grabbed his arm and started pulling him toward the shore.

"Whoa!" He laughed, and held back in the waist-high water. "I've got a problem you don't have to contend with, sugar. If I walk out on the beach right now, we're both going to be mighty embarrassed. I'd better just swim around for a minute and let things settle down."

With a wink he dove beneath the surface and came up ten yards away, cutting the water with his swift, powerful strokes. Abby watched him for a moment, lusting after that gorgeous body. Then with a shiver of anticipation she swam to shore, gathered their things and waited for him.

They drove up the coast and found a motel with a fishing pier, sailboats for rent and a vacancy sign flashing out front. Jack disappeared into the office and returned with a key and a devilish grin. "Got us a room with a waterfront view." He laughed, then kissed her throat. "I want this to be memorable!"

Abby giggled with happiness and sudden shyness. She pressed her cheek against his shoulder, her heart welling with love when he slipped an arm around her and held her. His brash enthusiasm softened to tenderness when he felt her tremble. He pulled the car into a parking spot, got out, and opened her door for her. "Come on, love," he whispered. "Don't be frightened."

"I'm not," she assured him, her curls scattering droplets of water as she shook her head. "I'm not scared. Just . . . dazzled!" And she laughed softly, her love shining in her eyes.

Jack kissed her nose and slipped the key in the lock. The door swung open, and, in a dance choreographed by Fate itself, Jack took her in his arms and carried her to the bed. He kissed her with heart-stopping sweetness, drew his hands down her body, and tugged her wet shorts down her thighs and legs. Abby stroked his back and shoulders, pressing kisses into the damp hair at the back of his neck. "I love you."

"I love you, too—and I *want* you so damn much I think I'm going to die!" He groaned and caught her face between his hands, then kissed her eyes, her nose, her cheeks and chin.

He grabbed the bottom edge of her T-shirt and pulled it up and off, leaving only the two narrow strips of bikini covering her golden body. And then, while she still had her arms stretched up over her head, he bent and kissed the firm, ripe rise of her breasts, then nipped at her nipples through the wet, slick fabric.

Abby yelped, laughing, feeling her body heat soar to the boiling point. Pressing her slim little hips against the taut bow of his body, she reached behind her and untied her bikini top. Before it drifted to the floor his hands already had captured her small, rose-tipped breasts, and then his mouth was where his hands had been. Abby moaned softly, swooning as his tongue rasped over her sensitive flesh.

Then her moans became cries of excitement as she fell back against the circle of his arms and felt his mouth traveling down across her body, tasting her, licking and nipping and kissing her. He sank to his knees, rubbing his face against her belly while she curved over him, kissing his hair, his shoulders, the back of his neck. He said her name, the sound muffled against her body, his voice thick and hoarse with desire. And then he pulled her down, slowly, letting all of her body fall against him, her thighs, belly, breasts sliding against his chest, his mouth dusting kisses across her skin and then locking on to her mouth as she folded to her knees on the floor.

Grabbing handfuls of his thick, shaggy hair, she pressed her mouth to his, hungry to kiss him, to taste him, to melt away and become part of him. She knew nothing, nothing would ever feel like this again—and that nothing else would *ever* be the same. And she was glad! Joy flamed in her. Passion burned. Excitement sizzled. Oh, other people could jump out of planes or leap off cliffs with only a rope, but she had this, this flying, leaping feeling of ecstasy within her.

"Jack!" She gasped, trembling and laughing and kissing him all at the same time. "Why did we wait so long?"

"Beats the hell out of me, sweetheart!" His strangled laughter became a groan, and he ripped off his clothes and pulled her flat down on top of him on the floor. Right on top of him she squirmed and wiggled her way out of the bikini bottom, only realizing how she was adding to his craziness when she felt the uncontrollable response of his naked body and heard the sharp intake of his breath. "Sorry," she said, and wiggled some more, kissing him all over his face and chest.

He groaned, holding her head between his hands and stilling her mouth only long enough to slip his tongue inside and kiss her with a tense, compelling fierceness.

She placed her hands on his chest, against the dark, curly hair and the hot skin. And she let the palms of her hands travel a slow journey all over him, learning him inch by inch. And he explored her length and silky secret places, pulling little moans and cries of delight out of her, and she drew her knees up alongside his hips and sat on him, trying to pin him there with her weight while she kissed his throat and chest. But with one touch he had her limp and trembling, gasping and laughing, and he rolled over on top of her, holding his weight up on his hands, grinning and asking and wanting and promising all without a word, and she answered without a word, sliding her hands down his back and drawing him down to her, taking his weight, his power, his strength, his love, taking everything he had and giving all of herself to him.

Later they lay sprawled across the king-size bed. Half in a daze, Abby looked down at their two bodies, their skin rippling gold and flame-bright, valleys shadowed, curves burnished, all ripeness and power, softness and strength. Leaning back, she pressed her hands flat against her breasts, and breathed, "So *this* is why I have this body. . . ."

"One reason—and a mighty nice one." Curving over her, he kissed the backs of both her hands, then lifted them and kissed her nipples. "Ummm, I do love you."

They drifted to sleep, and after an hour they woke within seconds of each other, as if there were some magic connection between them now.

Stretching, Jack untangled himself from the loose moorings of her cool, sweet limbs and walked to the window. The sky was the blue of Abby's eyes, and beneath it the sea was streaked with color, turquoise and azure and a pale, beckoning green. A flock of sailboats lay beached at the water's edge, sails the colors of crayons, all pointing into that perfect sky.

"Abby, let's go sailing!" he said, turning to smile at her.

She waved one languid hand, a wisp of a smile on her lips. "Ohhh, come on back to bed. . . ."

He strode back to her side and planted a kiss on each sleepy eyelid. "Have you ever done it on a sailboat?" he asked, a devilish light in his eyes.

She raised one brow. "I've hardly ever 'done it,' as you so gallantly phrase it, anywhere! Certainly not on a sailboat—"

"Then we have to! Come on." And he was laughing, kissing her breasts, pulling her out of bed all at once.

"Jack!" She gasped, giggling and wiggling in his arms. "Wait! Let's save something for tomorrow!"

"No. Let's do everything today!"

So in moments Abby was sitting snug against their knapsack in the bottom of a rented sailboat with a bright red sail, and Jack was whistling at the tiller as he steered them around a sandbar.

"You're a crazy man!" she called, loving the sure, easy brashness of the man.

"That's why you love me!" he said, winking, treasuring the tilt of her lovely, heart-shaped face and her smile of mock reprimand.

He let go of the tiller to plant a kiss on her mouth.

"Hey!" she shouted. "Keep both hands on the wheel, mister!"

"I want both hands on you, darlin'."

"You had your chance, Jack Gallagher, and you chose to go sailing. So sail!" But she came and sat next to him, wrapping her arm around his good, solid waist.

He brushed her hair back from her face and kissed her ear, the curve of her neck, the hollow of her throat. "Ummm. You are the most delicious woman."

"It's this salt air. Good for the appetite," she answered lightly.

They sailed for about an hour, up and down the coast, watching the fish play in the rolling swells of the Gulf. Abby lay facedown on the deck, mesmerized by her own happiness. She felt the brush of Jack's body against her own, listened to the off-key tune he whistled, smelled the pleasing, heat-baked mixture of salt, sweat, and suntan oil. She had never felt so totally relaxed, so complete, so alive.

"Where are we?" she murmured, wanting really only to hear the sound of his voice.

"We're out a bit, heading north. It's beautiful here, Abby. I can see why you love it."

"I love you. Only you," she murmured, smiling dazedly.

Jack laughed. "Love is supposed to broaden your horizons, darlin'," he said teasingly. "And talking about horizons, do I need to worry about those clouds?" He pointed out over the water.

Abby rolled onto her side, and then sat bolt upright. "Yikes! That's a real storm coming, Jack. We'd better get back."

"Hey, you've been promising rain since I got here, woman—"

"And here it comes! I mean it, Jack. You don't know how fast the storms roll in down here. It can be wild! They come off the Gulf or the Atlantic, pound across the peninsula, and then squall out to sea. Happens like clockwork every afternoon all summer, once they get started. And today looks like the day! We'd better hurry."

"Okay. Don't worry." Jack turned the little boat toward shore, tacking back and forth to catch the rising wind.

Abby's practiced eye watched the narrow line of clouds rise and darken, while Jack calmly headed the sailboat in. But for every inch he gained toward shore, the wind pushed him north another two.

"We're not going to make it in, Abby," he said. "I'm going to head for that island instead."

"Okay. Fine," she said, holding onto the edge of the boat.

Jack turned the boat and raced ahead of the storm, the sail straining, bellying out with the gusting wind. The first drops of rain, heavy as water balloons, splashed on their heads and shoulders. "That's rain that wants you to sit up and take notice!" Jack laughed. He drew a quick hand down her cheek. "Don't worry, darlin'. We'll be fine."

"I know," she said, worrying away. "I trust you."

He gave her a wink, and steered northeast as the squall line drew nearer, a solid curtain of rain that mocked the heavy, erratic drops that already had them both soaked. The boat leaped and jumped across the surface of the water, steadily closing the gap between them and the waiting island. As soon as the nose touched sand, Jack grabbed the bowline, jumped overboard, and yanked the boat up onto the sand.

Abby grabbed the knapsack and scrambled onto shore. Together they pulled the boat way up past the water line as the sky opened up: Rain as sharp as needles pelted their bare skin. "Ouch!" Abby yelped.

"Hey!" Jack shouted, laughing, holding his shirt over her drenched head. "I've never heard of rain that hurts!"

She glared at him and swore. "I am marooned on an island with a crazy man!"

Still laughing, he took her arm, and they raced toward a clump of pines and palms that offered the only hope of shelter. Underneath the trees it was wet but safe.

Leaning against the nearest trunk, Jack looked at Abby and grinned. "Made it!"

Abby punched him in the shoulder. "Oh, why do I always end up in these wild situations with you, Gallagher? And why do they always involve water!" She gasped, breathless and shaking like a leaf.

"Come here," he said, opening his arms.

"I don't want to 'come here.' " She frowned fiercely. "I wanted to 'come here' *back there*, safe in our nice, warm king-size bed in our nice air-conditioned room. I don't want to 'come here' in the middle of a rain squall, soaking wet, and probably lost to boot!"

Jack forced back his grin, but his dark eyes still flashed with excitement. "Think of it as an adventure, darlin'."

"I was *having* an adventure! and one a day is enough for me, Jack Gallagher!"

"One a day only counts for vitamins, darlin'. Making love's a different matter."

Suddenly she felt warm and delicious from her head to her toes, but she wasn't about to let on. "And who's talking about making love?" she demanded, fighting to keep from smiling.

"Me. Come on. Let's '*do it*' in the rain."

She started to laugh, and the laughter bubbled in her throat like champagne, with the same happy result. Dizzy, weak-kneed, she fell into his arms. "Okay, Gallagher, have it your way!"

They tumbled onto the wet, packed sand and made wild, passionate, abandoned love. The rain dripped through the palm fronds, rinsing off the sand that stuck to their arms and legs and backs and thighs and hair.

"Oooh, oh, Jack!" Abby gasped, writhing in ecstasy. "Oh, Jack . . ." And she was laughing and crying all at the same time. She wound her fingers into his hair, pressing her mouth to his, hoping to stifle the little love cries she couldn't restrain. What if someone was near? What if someone could hear her? And she was shaking with desire, shaking with a wild abandonment she had never known before. And always in her ear was Jack's soft "I love you . . . love you . . . love you" as he covered her face with kisses and filled her with love.

When she could breathe again, Abby lay on top of him, her body spread out peacefully across the solid beauty of his body. Jack smiled happily into her eyes and kissed the tip of her nose. "So—what do you think of lovemaking in the rain?"

"Rain was lovely," she murmured. "It's the *sand!*" She wrinkled her nose, laughing with the same luxurious happiness.

"Don't worry about the sand," he said softly. "I'll be your blanket, your bed, the place you come home to."

Afterward they went swimming naked in the sea. The rain had stopped and when the sun dipped toward the horizon they reluctantly climbed back into their suits and bailed out the little boat.

"So, Gallagher"—Abby smiled, perched on the bow of the boat as Jack unfolded a damp but still usable map—"can you get us back to civilization?"

"Unfortunately."

She laughed, walked over, and wrapped her arms around his neck. Pressing her slim body into the waiting curve of his, she kissed his chin. "What could be more romantic than a sunset sail? A perfect ending to a perfect day."

The sail back was calm and lovely. As they neared shore, the palms looked like silhouettes cut from thick black construction paper, pasted against a pale beach and an indigo sky. Lights were shining in the motel and glowing softly from lanterns strung across the wide wooden patio.

"Oh"—Abby sighed—"I'm going to hate to say goodbye to this place, this day—"

"Not yet, darlin'. We're staying the night." He caught her face between his hands and kissed the protests from her lips. "Abby, I need another day all alone with you. A long, loving night. A lazy morning. A hot, stormy afternoon. I can't take you back yet. I just can't!"

"Oh, I'm glad!" Abby cried. "I feel the same way. But—but I have to go back. I have to get to the Websters' farmers' market in the morning."

"Let Jeanette do it for you," Jack answered with maddening surety. "You do enough for her."

"But she has summer school, and—"

"And *nothing*. Two classes. She can handle it."

Abby frowned, torn by the emotions warring in her heart. "I don't know . . ." she whispered, biting her lips. "What if—"

"I don't care about 'what ifs,' " Jack insisted, kissing her neck. "I only care about us."

"But—"

Calmly, Jack straightened, giving the tiller a smooth, controlled turn. The motel swung around behind them, and ahead was the open sea.

"Jack!" Abby gasped. "What are you doing?"

"If you want to see land again, I think you'd better say yes." His grin glinted in the growing darkness.

"That's blackmail, Jack Gallagher! You wouldn't want my affection on those terms."

"On *any* terms, darlin'! So—what do you say?"

"I say you're impossible. Stubborn, outrageous—" She looked at the steely determination of his stance, the wonderful width of his shoulders, the sweet, irresistible joy of his smile. "Wellll . . . I guess we deserve another day. As long as you promise it will be as wonderful as today."

"I promise, Abby," he said softly, and brought the boat to shore.

When they were back in the motel room, Jack walked to the big bed, with its cool white sheets. He pulled the blanket back and winked at her. "Come here. . . ."

Eight

"Oh, look what you've done to me, Jack! For the first time in my life I don't want to go back to work. I don't want to see the Paradise Café. Paradise is *here!*" Wearing nothing but a smile, Abby snuggled in Jack's arms.

Jack ran his hands lovingly down her silken back and cupped her round little bottom, then pulled her even closer. "You're not going to get an argument from me, darlin'. I'm a happy man."

Abby nuzzled playfully under his chin. She kissed the strong, steady pulse at his throat, brushed her lips over his collarbone, and pressed kisses into the thick, dark hair on his chest. "Ummm. Now I know what they mean by contentment. Oh, Jack, I thought it was something everyone in the world but me would know. I thought I'd spend my whole life wanting more, working harder, struggling after some dream. But this—this is lovely." She lifted herself up on one elbow, smiled into his dark eyes, and drew a finger down the sharp angle of his jaw. "You know, you're beautiful."

He shook his head, looking at her with tolerant amusement. "Me? Nope, too big and burly. But you,

you're all the colors of summer: Golden skin, corn-flower-blue eyes, the blush of a peach on your cheeks." His hands began to touch each place his words described. "And your nipples are dusty rose, this sweet tangle of fur is the color of ripe wheat, the inside of your thighs is pale as cream. . . ."

"Oh, don't—don't stop!" she whispered, made bold and reckless by desire.

"Don't intend to, darlin'. " Smiling, he rolled on top of her. He covered her with his hard, loving body and loved her long and hard.

When ecstasy had subsided to a mere whimper of satiated pleasure, Abby peeked out from beneath her lashes.

Jack was lying next to her, one arm cocked under his head, watching her. His eyes darkened to smoke, and he reached out and stroked her bare flank. "I never thought I'd be the one to say this, but we'd better be heading back."

"I don't want to." Abby sighed and snuggled down against the pillow.

Jack laughed softly and kissed the tip of her nose. "I don't want to either, but I've got to check in with Pop and Bear, and someone I know has to be at work tomorrow."

He got out of bed, then reached down to offer her a hand.

Abby shook her head. "Nope, I'm not going." She pulled the covers up to her chin and lay there, her shining eyes daring him to make her move.

"You *are* a little nut! Get on out of there, Abby. Come morning you'll be chewing me out for not getting you home in time—"

"I won't. I promise! You don't think about Colo-rado, and I won't think about the café. We'll do nothing but sip piña coladas, lie in the sun, and make love."

Jack stared down at her, torn between amuse-ment and desire. "If I thought you meant one word of it, I'd be back in that bed before you could say Buck Rogers."

"How about 'buck naked'?" Abby drawled. She patted the bed next to her. "Come here!"

Settling his hands on his lean hips, Jack laughed. "You'll be sorry, woman."

"Not me! You're looking at a new Abby Clarke."

Something flickered in Jack's eyes. He rocked back on his heels and said softly, "But I'm happy with the old Abby Clarke."

Abby popped upright, wrapping her arms around her knees and looking up at him with sudden seriousness. "Are you? Really? *I* think she tends to be sort of a stick-in-the-mud—always worrying about something, always too busy to have fun. . . ." She let the words drift away, but her wide blue eyes were full of questions.

Jack brushed the hair back from her cheek with a gentle hand. "Now, I'm not saying she couldn't use a *little* loosening up"—he winked—"but I do love that girl."

"You do?" She flashed a bright, heart-stopping smile. "Well, then, I'd better keep her around. And *she* does have to be at work in the morning. By seven! So when we get to my place, you'd better go on home so I can get a decent night's sleep and—"

Laughing, Jack pulled her up into his arms. "I'm a good-hearted guy, not an angel." And to prove it he kissed her back into a sweet delirium before he drove her home.

He stayed the night but let her sleep, wrapped in his arms, her old quilt pulled lightly over them both. And he stayed in bed when she awoke at six, lay there watching her dress and brush her hair, watching her move around the narrow trailer. He loved every gesture, every sure, quiet movement. Before she left she came and kissed him lightly on the lips. "Stay asleep. I'll see you later." She hurried to the door, then hurried back. "I love you," she whispered.

"I love you too." He pulled her down for a quick kiss, holding her close for a moment, then let her go.

When he caught up with her at the Paradise Café about four that afternoon, she was up to her ears in business. There were boxes of produce covering the counter tops, a man delivering fresh snapper and grouper dropping ice shavings across her kitchen floor, a plumber fooling with something under the sink. And the rain was pounding on the windows.

Jack pushed the door all the way open and squeezed into the kitchen. At the sight of him, dripping wet, his shirt plastered to his gorgeous chest, Abby forgot about the plumber and fish seller and flew to Jack's arms and hugged him tight. "Oh, am I glad to see you! It's craziness here, and for a minute I was afraid I had only dreamed you."

He held her at arm's length and gave her a slow, steady smile. "No dream. Not one bit of it; not the sailboat, not the rain, not the sand and the—"

"Shh!" She smoothed the front of her skirt. "So—what have you been up to all day?"

"Met a fellow from the Florida game commission, and I tagged along. There was a twelve-foot alligator taking a stroll across a parking lot in Tavares on his way to Lake Dora, and we sort of helped him on his way."

"Oh, Jack, that's so dangerous! I wish you wouldn't fool around with things like that. Why can't you go to Disney World, like any other tourist?"

"If I were any other tourist, you wouldn't love me the way you do."

Laughter popped out of her. "'Oh—and how do I love you?'"

"Madly." He grabbed her around the waist and pulled her to him.

Abby wiggled away, casting a mortified glance around the kitchen. "Jack!"

Jack just shook his head. "Always worrying. I'll see you later, darlin'."

"Wait. Are you limping? Yes, you're limping, Jack Gallagher, you *are!* Now, don't you leave before you tell me what the hell happened."

"Nothing happened."

"Ahhh," came a snide drawl from the dining-room door. "What modesty. What courage." Simon was leaning there, an empty plastic glass dangling from one hand. "Bet she'll kiss it for you an' make it better."

"You can k—" Jack leaped forward, his hands balled into fists at his sides. Through the deadly humming in his ears he heard the others' gasps of dismay, Abby's muffled cry. So he stepped back and dropped a hand on Simon's shoulder.

Simon squirmed, but Jack's grip was iron, unshakable. "Hey, let go! You ruin this suit and you'll be sorry. I've got friends you wouldn't like!" he threatened.

Jack laughed in his face. "That's not hard to believe. I don't even like you." His smile faded. "So watch your manners, okay?"

Jack released his grip, and Simon jerked away and staggered through the back door. "And don't expect me back to help with dinner, either! You can do it yourself!" He turned, bumped heavily into a delivery man, then weaved on around to the driveway.

Jack shrugged. "Sorry. If you're short of help now for tonight, I'll go clean up and come on back."

Abby shook her head. "No. Really," and she laughed that nervous little laugh that comes on the tail end of tension. "No, it's easier without him." She turned as she heard the grinding sound of an engine refusing to come to life. "But I don't think he should drive now."

"I'll take care of it," Jack said.

"Ms. Clarke, I've got your tomatoes here," the newest intruder interrupted from the doorway. "Want to take a look?"

"Jack . . ." Abby sighed, letting her forehead fall against his broad chest.

He put his hands on her shoulders. "Go look at your tomatoes, sweet thing. And call if you need me. I'll see you later."

Abby smiled, rolled her eyes heavenward, and began checking the tomatoes, glad for an opportunity to concentrate on something other than Jack.

Coming home at midnight, she saw the soft glow of a lamp in her living room and raced up the steps. Jack was waiting in the trailer, his chair pushed back on two legs, his feet propped on the couch, reading a Florida Game and Fresh Water Fish Commission report on alligators. There was a warm wind blowing through the open window.

"Are you okay?" he asked, looking up as she came in. His eyes were dark with worry.

"Fine." She smiled. "We had a good night; no more problems. But I forgot how hard it is. Those two days spoiled me, Gallagher, so it's *your* fault."

"Then come here," he said, and he let the paper fall to the floor.

"Oh, no." She groaned, then laughed. "I haven't got the strength."

He chuckled. "No, silly. Just come over here. Sit down. Now, put your feet in my lap." And without another word he began to massage her feet, his strong hands working the tiredness right out of her. She leaned back, eyes closed, dreamy with pleasure.

When he stopped, thinking she was asleep, she wiggled her toes and gave him a mischievous little grin. "Can I have some more, please, sir?"

He massaged her feet, then trailed his hands up her calves, soothing, mesmerizing her, slowly moving his hands to her knees, her thighs. . . . Then, catching her ankles in one hand, he swung her legs up onto the couch, pressed her shoulders down to the other side, and lowered his sweet, welcomed weight down on top of her.

"Ah," she whispered happily, "that's better than any blanket yet invented by mankind!"

Almost another week vanished that way: Busy days apart, loving nights together.

One night when she came in, Jack was on the phone, talking to Pop, in Colorado. She fixed herself a cup of chamomile tea and sat down with a book, yet she couldn't help but hear the strain in Jack's voice. Like a thin, sharp knife, panic stabbed at her heart.

As soon as he hung up, she slipped into his arms. "So how are things?"

There was tension in his arms, in his voice. "I'm staying away too long, Abby. I've got to go back. There are things I need to take care of—"

"No! Oh, not yet. Please," she whispered, snuggling against his chest, "please?"

"Okay, darlin'. Shh, don't worry."

Saturday night he picked her up after closing and took her back to the houseboat, and on Sunday morning they lingered late in bed, kissing, snuggling, talking.

"I want you to stop worrying about that partner of yours, Abigail Jean," Jack said, kissing her eyelids.

"Would if I could," she answered softly. "I guess I've gotten myself into something I don't know how to get out of."

"What would it take?" he asked.

"A fairy godmother. A magic wish. A suitcase full of unmarked money." She laughed. "You happen to have any of the above on you, Gallagher?"

Lifting the cover, he grinned. "What you see is what you get, darlin'." But then he was serious again. He tightened his arms around her and held her close. "Let me talk to him. I'll straighten him out."

"Oh no, Jack!" she exclaimed, aghast at the thought. "I can handle it. Really. Besides, I want him polite, not dead."

"I wouldn't touch him."

"You wouldn't have to. One growl and he'd croak on the spot. But really"—she tugged at a handful of hair on his bronzed chest—"I'll take care of it."

"All right, if you say so," he agreed reluctantly. "Then on to the next piece of business—"

"I thought *I* was the next piece of business." She wriggled happily within his arms.

"That's pure pleasure," he whispered, then drew a deep breath. "Abby, I've got to go back to Colorado."

"No, I won't let you!" she said insistently, wrapping her arms tightly around his neck.

He gently cupped her face in his hands and kissed her mouth. "I've got to go, Abby. There's a five o'clock flight, and I've got to be on it."

She suddenly felt breathless, as if a terrible weight had settled on her chest. "But, Jack, can't you stay awhile longer?"

"They need me, Abby."

"So do I! I didn't want to. But you followed me here, and now I do! So it's not *fair* for you to leave." She stopped, dismayed at what her passion had led her to say. She knew she was being selfish. "I'm sorry, Jack," she said, fumbling for control, "I know you have to go. I understand." She rolled over to the side of the bed, bit her lip, and peeked up at him. "But you can't make me like it."

Jack forced a smile. "I don't like it either. But I'll be back as soon as I can. I promise."

She took him to the airport early, using the beach traffic as an excuse. The truth was, it hurt too much to watch the minutes tick by. She walked him to the gate, held back the tears while he kissed her, even managed to send him off with a smile. Then he was gone, vanished into the plane, into his mountains, into a world she had no control over. She dropped down into one of the plastic seats and started to cry, ignoring the stares of everyone around. And then, in the middle of a sob, she felt herself lifted out of her chair.

"Damn, woman, I can't do it. They'll have to manage a little longer without me." And Jack picked her up and strode out of the airport.

She cooked him all her favorite foods that night, topping dinner off with a strawberry shortcake that they took to bed with them. "Oh, Jack, I'm so glad you're here," she said, then tried to show some appropriate concern. "Will they manage okay, Bear and Pop?"

"Well, I spent an hour on the phone and got some of it worked out. That couple from Kansas City has fallen in love with the place. I told Pop to let them stay on free for another month, in exchange for helping out with the front desk, so that takes the pressure off him. And he just dug out a smoky-quartz crystal he thinks is good enough to sell to a museum, so he's flying high."

"But you miss him. I can tell," she whispered, stung with guilt.

"Yes. But I'd miss you more." He popped a strawberry into her mouth.

"And Bear?" she asked, licking whipped cream off his fingers.

"Oh, Bear says the rafting business is doing fine without me. Besides, there's a race this weekend, and with me out here, he'll probably come in first, so he's happy."

"I'm glad he's happy. Are you happy?" She threw one bare leg over his and snuggled close.

"Yes."

"How happy?" she asked, leaning over to kiss the tight band of muscle across his stomach.

"Very happy." He grinned.

Her kisses were butterflies flitting across his belly and chest, landing here . . . there. . . . "Just very happy?"

"Ecstatic!"

The next day Abby was at the Websters' farmers' market doing battle over the price of sweet corn.

"Henry, it's already one o'clock, and you want to get out of this heat as much as I do!" she said with a groan, wiping her damp forehead on her dusty forearm. "Three cents less a dozen or I'm going over to Randy's stand!"

"Randy picked that corn three days ago! You'll never buy it, Abby Clarke."

She strode away, glanced at the corn and strode back. "Two cents less, Henry."

"Penny and a half, and you take all I've got."

"Done."

She drove the pickup to a space behind the stand, raising a long, slow trail of dust that sifted down on the children eating hot boiled peanuts under the trees, and backed into the nearest space. She had just finished loading the heavy crates when Jack appeared.

"Great timing, Gallagher! Where were you when I needed you?" She gave him a tired smile and accepted the ice-cold bottle of cola he held out to her. "Umm—you're forgiven! How did you find me?"

"It's Monday, isn't it?" He kissed the tip of her nose, leaving one clean spot on her dusty face. Laughing, he dropped an arm across her narrow shoulders and hugged her close. "Come on, let me drive you back to the Paradise, and then we'll go for a swim."

Abby climbed gratefully into the passenger seat of

the pickup and took another long, refreshing pull on the bottle of cola. Then her eyes narrowed. "Hey, what about your car?"

"I got a ride out here with that fellow from fish and game."

"Oh, no, Jack, not 'gators again!"

"Me?" Jack asked, feigning innocence.

"Don't waste your time, Gallagher. That boy-scout look isn't going to work on me! I want you here, but I want you in one piece."

"Abby, I'm just going along for the ride—"

"You? No chance! You're always right in the thick of things, good or bad! And you don't know 'gators." She folded her arms across her chest and glared at him.

"Hey, stop worrying. I really am just going along to watch. They've had a report of a big 'gator in a lake down near Orlando. Trouble is, there are houses built all around the lake and a couple of small dogs have disappeared, so the neighbors are getting worried. We're just going down tonight—"

"Tonight? Then I'm coming along."

"That's the spirit!" He playfully squeezed her knee. "I'm glad you want to watch!"

"Watch, ha! I'm going to pray."

When they drove down that evening, the Florida Game and Fresh Water Fish Commission truck was already parked near the lake. It was a pretty little community, with houses dotting the lakeshore, and neighbor connected to neighbor by a network of landscaped bicycle and jogging paths.

"Funny place for an alligator to end up," Jack said musingly, pulling his Jeep in next to the truck.

"The alligators were here first," Abby corrected, looking around. "There's probably a 'gator in every patch of water in Florida. The trouble is, there are more and more people staking claim to those same patches of water, and in the spring and early summer they all run into each other, because the 'gators are out hunting and looking for mates."

"Sure. Blame it on love!"

"Gallagher . . ." She groaned, and gave him a shove.

"And how do you know so much about alligators, Ms. Clarke?"

"I'm a native, remember? A rarer breed than the 'gator, these days."

"Rare and wonderful, I'd say." Jack smiled and edged along the seat to her side, then put his arms around her.

"Is this the condemned man's last wish?" Abby asked, then pursed her lips for a kiss.

Jack laughed out loud. "Are you trying to tell me something, darlin'?"

"Well, just remember: You don't have to swim faster than the 'gator. Just faster than the fellow in the water with you."

"Very funny!"

"Old Florida alligator joke," she said, shrugging. Then she touched his cheek. "Just be careful, Jack. Please."

At that moment the door to the truck opened, and the game warden climbed out. He was wearing a vest over his khaki uniform, a gun in a holster, and a sort of miner's cap, with the lamp already shining brightly in the dusk. And he was holding something that looked like a rifle with a coil of rope attached. "Hey, Jack, glad you could make it."

"Hey, Dave. This is Abby Clarke. She's going to watch."

"Great. She can join the crowd." He jerked his head toward the sidelines.

And sure enough, a crowd had materialized out of the dusk. Mothers and children, teenagers, fathers just home from work and still wearing their suits and ties, a man positioning a camera on a tripod, and others with cameras and binoculars at the ready were gathered along the shore. There, a safe distance from the water's edge, they could catch all the action.

"They must think we're going to put on a show," Dave said, laughing without much humor. "Actually we're going to do this real fast, and real careful. A 'gator is one dangerous animal, quick and mean. And from what the reports read, this one could be twelve feet and five hundred pounds."

"Oh, Jack," Abby whispered, feeling suddenly faint.

Jack put an arm around her waist. "Abby, it's going to be fine."

"You bet it is." Dave grinned. "I've done this a dozen times and never lost a piece of me yet. Twenty –thirty minutes, and we'll be back. Gonna find that 'gator, shoot it with this." He hefted the rifle/lariat contraption. "This, here, gets hooked in the hide, and the 'gator thinks it can get away by rollin' and rollin' around and instead winds itself up in the rope. We tow it in, tie it up, and take it away.'"

"Hell of a way to earn a living." Jack's eyes glinted with anticipation.

"Hell of a way!" Dave agreed, grinning in the dark.

"Did either of you ever think of selling used cars?" Abby asked, hands on hips.

The two men laughed. Then, in a voice rough-edged with excitement, Dave said to Jack, "Ready? Let's get the boat and hunt up a 'gator."

Abby watched the rowboat move out onto the dark lake, leaving a wake silvered by moonlight. Her heart was in her throat. She was really scared, far more scared than she had let on. *Damn that Jack Gallagher, damn him—No! I don't mean that. Keep him safe, please.*

She heard the steady pull of the oars. Silence. Frogs. Silence. The boat moved from one cluster of reeds to another, in and out of the tall grasses and lily pads. The beam of light from Dave's cap jumped around the lake, landing here and there like some giant firefly. There was the sound of rowing, then silence, then a sudden shout and splash, and more shouting, and the sound of a gun and wild splashing and thrashing, and more shouts, and silence. Silence. Frogs and silence. Then the boat pulled into view, both men bent over the oars, and Abby could see that a huge alligator was lashed to the side, a loop of rope tying tight its fierce jaws, its teeth showing like rows of daggers, its eyes unblinking.

"Stand back. Everyone stand back!" Dave yelled, quite unnecessarily, since the crowd had already backed away onto the safety of someone's neatly mowed lawn. He and Jack bent against the weight and dragged the alligator out of the water. Carefully, holding to rope and tail, they tied him again with a second length of rope, then hoisted him into the truck.

"Big 'gator!" Dave said, grinning.

"Great 'gator!" Jack agreed, wearing the same grin.

Abby slumped against Jack's Jeep, wet with the sweat of nervousness. She didn't know whether to jump up and cheer or sit down and cry.

Jack winked at her and stepped closer. "Told you everything would be fine. That was some 'gator, wasn't it!" He gave her that boyish, daredevil grin of his, his broad chest heaving with labored breaths. "Some 'gator . . ."

"You're crazy, Gallagher," Abby said, rolling her eyes heavenward. "You're too much for me, sometimes."

"Long as it's only sometimes." He laughed and touched her face.

"Hey, Romeo," Dave shouted. "You'd better go take care of that leg. Nearest hospital's right on 436. Just head east, about—"

"I know where it is!" Abby yelled. "But what happened?"

Jack pulled open the Jeep door. "Why don't you drive, Abby?"

Abby froze, mouth open wide, eyes open wide.

"Abby, it's nothing. Just climb in and we'll drive over. Or go around the other side and I'll drive."

Gulping air, gasping, Abby choked out, "Did it bite you? Did the 'gator—"

There was a gasp from the crowd.

"Shhh. Everything's fine," he said loudly, then pushed her into the driver's seat of the Jeep and climbed in on the other side. "Everything's fine, Abby. Don't worry. Just put it into reverse, and let's get out of here."

Abby jerked the car into motion and raced down the road. "You'd better tell me what's happening, Jack Gallagher, before I strangle you, and then you won't *need* a hospital!"

"The alligator didn't touch me," he said, holding back his smile in the face of her fury. "Set a leg out to get our balance, and something bit me. Think it was a snake—"

"Snake!"

"Water moccasin," he admitted. "But we have plenty of time to get to a hospital. Nothing's going to happen. Don't worry."

"You tell me not to worry one more time and I'm going to hit you over that thick head of yours with this gearshift," she threatened, yanking it into fourth. "Why couldn't we stay home and watch 'Scarecrow and Mrs. King,' like other couples? Or go on a date. Bowling. Get drunk at a bar. Oh, how long has it been?"

"Just a few minutes."

"Oh, God . . ."

"We have plenty of time. Don't worry."

She raced down the highway, weaving in and out of traffic, keeping one eye on Jack.

In about five minutes he began to sweat. She saw the perspiration pop out along his forehead and upper lip.

"You okay?"

"Fine," he said, gritting his teeth. He patted her knee, then clenched his hand on his own thigh, digging his fingers into his leg as if to tear out the pain. "Whoa—I think I do have a bit of a problem here."

"Oh, Jack," she said with a gasp, "what's it feel like now?"

"You don't want to know," he said, sucking air through clenched teeth.

His face had gone from white to gray, and she could see him fighting back waves of nausea.

"Here we are! Hang on!" She swung into the emergency entrance and drove up to the door, the frantic pounding of her heart drowned out by the steady blare of her horn.

The doctor told Abby they would have to keep Jack in the hospital two or three days.

And it's a good thing, too, Jack Gallagher! Abby swore, *because if I could get my hands on you, I'd murder you!*

She blinked fast, furious at him, too furious to let herself cry at the sight of his being rolled out of the ER on a stretcher.

"Abby," he said softly, stopping the orderly with a look and lifting onto his elbows. "Abby, I'm fine. They gave me a shot of antivenin, and everything's okay—"

"Everything's *not* okay, Gallagher. This was stupid. Unnecessary. Here you are, not anywhere near a raft or a river, and you're still taking chances!" She swallowed hard, blinking madly. She shook her head, and locked her arms across her chest.

Jack started to climb off the stretcher, but the orderly pushed him back. "Hold it, buddy. You're supposed to keep off the leg."

"Forget the leg," Jack snapped, then sank back,

exhausted. "Abby." His voice dropped to an intimate whisper. "Abby, I'm sorry. Come here." He held out his hand.

Abby turned away. She hurried down the long hallway, shoulders hunched forward, seeing nothing. But she heard Jack, heard him call, "Abby, I love you," felt the words fall like shards of glass on her unforgiving back.

She pushed through the door out into the dark night. When she got to the Jeep, she put her head down on the steering wheel and wept. "Why, oh, why, can't things ever be simple for me? Why can't anything be easy?" She cried for a while, until finally the tension was gone, as well as the fear, the anger, the self-pity.

Blowing her nose, she caught sight of herself in the rearview mirror. "Nice going, Abigail," she muttered. "You dope! Didn't even tell him you love him. What if something happened to him tonight? What if the antivenin didn't work? What if . . . what if . . ." She pressed her hands to her pounding head. "Oh, I'm tired of 'what ifs.' Why can't he just be like everyone else? Why can't he be safe and sensible? Why can't *I*?"

Again tears stung her eyes, and she drove home slowly, exhausted.

She opened the trailer door and let it slam tinnily behind her; its echo ricocheted through the empty night. Pushing the cats away, she sloughed off her clothes. In a moment she had fallen across the bed and was lost in a troubled sleep.

Nine

She slept right through the alarm the next morning, and only woke when the cats wrapped themselves around her neck, meowing in hunger. "Holy moly— nine-thirty!" she yelped. She jumped in and out of the shower. Threw cat food in the dirty dish. Grabbed her shoes, purse, keys, and raced out the door, still buttoning her blouse.

When she got to the Paradise, a box of snapper was leaking ice water on the step. Dragging it inside, she paused just long enough to scrawl "Today's Special: Blackened Snapper with Mangoes" on the blackboard over the counter and scurried into the kitchen.

The first customers arrived before she had finished lunch preparations, and she offered free limeades and boiled peanuts as pacifiers.

"Hurry up, Archie. Take this out to table four!" She pushed a bowl into his hands.

"Don't yell at me! It's not my fault the lunchtime waiter didn't show, and I was on time, even if it looks like someone else around here wasn't."

"Archie, please, I am not in the mood for any back talk."

"I wasn't back-talking. No, sirree. I was just stating the facts, and wondering why certain people are awfully edgy lately—"

"Archie!"

"I'm gone. Yes, ma'am, takin' this right out there. And no back talking."

When the lunch crowd cleared out and her helpers were sitting in the dining room having their own lunch, Simon came in. "So, what was the take today?"

Abby drew a long hiss of a breath through clenched teeth. "I don't know what the *take* was. I only know I've been cleaning, sautéing, and serving snapper all morning long, and I could have used a little help! You know, Simon, a little help would have been real nice. We *are* partners, aren't we?"

He met her exasperated question with a nasty grin. "You bet we are, kiddo. But I'm the money; you're the elbow grease." He laughed at her swift flash of anger. "And that's the way *you* wanted it, remember?" He pointed one narrow, manicured finger at her. "You're the one who wanted total say in the kitchen. This was *your* place, *your* precious Paradise Café. Well"—he shrugged, suddenly bored with the argument—"it doesn't look like you're having much fun in paradise right now."

"Simon, you are not a nice person." Abby shook her head and closed her eyes.

Color burned in his face, edging his lips with white. "Well, maybe I'm not Sir Galahad, like your mountain man, but I'm the real world, baby. I'm *your* real world! And maybe you'd better start paying some close attention, instead of dreamin' and romancin'!"

Abby tipped up her chin. "That's none of your business."

"Just trying to be helpful."

"Baloney, Simon. You wouldn't offer help if the place were on fire." Her blond hair was sweat-dark, and was clinging to her cheeks and neck. "Go away, Simon. Just go away," she said wearily.

"I'll go if I want, and I'll stay if I want, and you don't have a thing to say about it."

That was the last straw! "Like hell I don't! This is still my place. I'm the one who makes it work. You'd look pretty dumb investing in an empty restaurant, with nothing cooking on the stove and not a customer in sight!"

"Not half as dumb as you'd look, locked out of your own sweet little Paradise Café, with all your friends and neighbors watching. You see, *I* don't give a damn about this place, your fine cooking, your big plans: The mortgage on your parents' house, that savings account for your little sister. Oh, I know all about it! Hell, if this place goes bust, I'll just write it off as a tax loss. But *you*—you'll be back on the porch of some little cracker shack, shelling peanuts."

Abby gasped, her face as white as if he had struck her. She stared at him, speechless with shock, as he left.

Alone, she tried not to cry, but the tears choked her throat, burned her eyes, and then she was sobbing, muffling her face in a tea towel. How could this be happening? How could she have made such a mistake? Why hadn't someone warned her or helped her? Why didn't anyone help her now? *Oh, Jack, why aren't you here when I need you?*

And then, like an impossible answer to a prayer, she heard the front door open.

"Jack?" she cried, knowing it couldn't be, but wishing it anyway. "Jack, is that—"

"It's me. Jeanette," her sister called, heading for the kitchen.

Abby rubbed her face dry, grabbed a pot, and started scrubbing.

"Wow, looks like a tornado touched down in there. Where's your waiter? Can I give you a hand?"

Keeping her back turned, Abby attempted a cheerful "Sure, that would be great. Thanks, sis."

Jeanette stopped. "Are you all right?"

"Sure. Fine."

The younger girl came closer and peeked over her sister's shoulder. "Hey, you've been crying."

"Onions," Abby answered hastily.

"Huh-uh, those aren't onion tears! Oh, Abby, what's the matter?" Her sister's unlikely show of weakness had her scared. "What happened? Did you and Jack have a fight?"

"No. It's Simon. We had a—a small business disagreement."

"Oh." Jeanette sighed with relief. "Is that all? Well, why don't you go find Jack and get some good hugs? You'd feel better in no time!"

Abby just closed her eyes, pressing one hand to her damp forehead. "Sometimes it is hard to believe that we are sisters, Jeanette."

"I know. It takes me back at times too." She laughed. "But anyway, I'm sorry that creep gave you a bad time. Would a hug from me help?"

"A hug is not what I need!"

"See, that's where you're wrong. Hugs help. Hugs and kisses are even better. And some good, strong arms wrapped around you can sure feel good. Now, I," she added quickly, seeing Abby's eyes widen, "am speaking only from what I see in the movies, you understand. But you, Abby, you've got the real thing!"

"For all the good it does." Abby sighed.

"You have to give it a chance, Abby. You have to be willing to admit you can't do everything, that you need someone," Jeanette insisted with quiet sincerity. "So why don't you let me mind the store, and you go find Jack."

"Oh, he's easy to find. He's in the hospital. He went 'gator hunting and got himself bitten by a water moccasin."

"Oh, no!" Jeanette gasped. "Is he okay? Where did he get bitten? Was it awful? How big a snake? Did you get to stay with him all night?"

"Jeanette, take it easy. He'll be fine—"

"But I can't *stand* it. He's so wonderful, and if anything happened to him, I—I—" She started to cry, and suddenly Abby found herself crying again too.

"Oh, sis, don't, please!" Jeanette said. "Here, have a tissue. Sit down. I'll call Jack for you."

And before Abby could answer, Jeanette was dialing information for the hospital number, which she just as quickly dialed. "Hi! Mr. Gallagher, please. Jack Gallagher. No, I don't know the room number—"

"Two-sixteen," Abby whispered, but her sister was already talking again.

"Hello, Jack? . . . No, it's Jeanette, but Abby's right here. . . . Yeah, hold on, but are you okay? I almost died when Abby told me! Was it awful? You're so brave. I couldn't stand even thinking about your being hurt, and— Yeah, that's okay. Sure, I'll put her on. You be good, now, ya hear!"

Abby took the phone. "Hi, Jack. . . . Oh, I'm fine; don't worry about me. How are you? You're really all right? And the swelling went down? Can you walk? . . . Oh, I bet that's a sight!" She gave a hiccupy little laugh. "Jack, when can you come home?"

She listened to the low, husky sound of his voice, letting it fill her from her toes to the top of her head. Everything else disappeared, the way everyday sounds fade when you hold a shell to your ear and the roar of the sea encompasses you. All her hard edges melted, and she felt warm and alive, happy for the first moment that day.

"What?" she asked, brought back to reality. "I'm sorry, what did you say? . . . day after tomorrow? Yes, oh yes, I'll be there! Maybe I can even sneak over before the dinner rush, if I can get caught up, and if—what?" She laughed softly, an easy little laugh aimed at herself. "I guess I *am* running in ten directions at once again, but—but I suddenly had this awful need to see you."

His answer made her blush. "I love you too," she whispered, and hung up the phone.

Jeanette was grinning at her. "Didn't I tell you about hugs?"

"Okay, little sister, for once, you were right. Just don't let it go to your head. Now, I've got to get started on this evening's menu. Let's see, there's the puff pastry to do, and then Lena can shell the peas, and . . . Hey! Would you run down into Zellwood and get me a couple of bushels of white corn? Oh, Jeanette, everything's going to be all right."

At eight-thirty Wednesday morning Abby was standing in front of her half-steamed bathroom mirror, blowing her hair dry, thinking of Jack and grinning at herself like a giddy teenager.

Jack . . . Jack . . . Jack. It was the sound her heart made as it pounded in her throat. There, she could see her own pulse, its wild fluttering beneath her skin. *Jack.* In a few minutes she would see him, touch him. Oh, she'd touch him, all right. She'd make up for her silly anger the other night at the hospital. And she'd tell him—no! she'd *show* him— how much she really did love him, and she'd make him forget all her mistakes. I mean, a person couldn't change all at once, right? And she had spent so many years holding back that it was hard to let go all of a sudden. But she would! She *could,* and she'd *prove it,* and—

There was a loud knock at the screen door.

Jeanette? Now, that girl was supposed to be home. *I'll murder her if she's come to tag along, and I don't care how crazy she is about Jack!*

Aloud she yelled, "Okay, okay, I'm coming!" She

pulled the door open. "Jeanette? Oh, Harry! And Mr. Wyler! What a surprise. What is it?"

"Can we talk to you a minute, Abby?"

"Well, I—I was just on my way out."

Harry Griffin tugged the bill down on his baseball cap, stuffed his hands in his pockets, and shifted his feet on the tiny front step. "It's kind of important, if you could spare a minute."

The air went out of her balloon with a hiss. "Sure, Harry, Mr. Wyler, you all come in and sit down. Let me get you a cup of coffee."

"No, thanks, we won't trouble you for anything."

The two men remained standing, looking at the floor.

"Thing is," Harry, the official spokesman, said, "we want to know why you canceled our deliveries after all these years, and without even a word or a howdy-do."

Abby blinked. "Canceled my orders? Me? I don't know what you mean. I *mean*"—she laughed, shaking her head in disbelief—"I can't run the Paradise without chicken and fish!"

Neither man cracked a smile.

Abby dropped into a chair. "Please. Sit down. Now, tell me what's going on."

"I got a letter yesterday saying you'd no longer be doing business with me."

"That's right," Wyler echoed.

" 'We're taking our business elsewhere at a fairer price' were the exact words," he quoted, angrily meeting her eyes. "Not what I expected from an old friend."

"We *are* old friends! And you must know I'd never do that. If I had to cancel an order, you know I'd talk to you in person! But I didn't cancel anything!"

"Your partner did. Sent it with a bank check, right to the penny. And a copy to your lawyers, it said. Any future deliveries would be returned at my expense."

"That's right," came the echo.

"Well, ignore it!" Abby snapped. "Damn that man." She pressed her fingertips to her temples. Then she looked up, cold-eyed and determined. "Harry, Mr. Wyler, I'm sorry about this. But you just go on delivering my orders, and I'll take care of this mix-up. And I apologize for the confusion." She stood up and offered her hand. "Thanks for coming over."

"Uh—Abby, you might want to give Gebbaurer a call if, I mean, if you want to keep using Sumter Laundry. He—uh, he got the same letter." The man was stammering, uncomfortable to be telling her things she obviously didn't know about her own business.

And Abby felt sick. Sick and embarrassed. Shamed before these men who had watched her build the Paradise up from nothing, friends who had respected and encouraged her.

Keeping her head up, she walked over to the phone and picked up a pad and pencil. "Who else? Who else had I better call?"

She made seven calls that morning, apologizing, explaining. Her whole body was shaking with the frustration she kept hidden as she spoke. Her voice was calm, steady, reassuring, but her stomach was clenching and unclenching like a fist. The last call was to Simon. His answering machine was on, and when she was done with her message she hoped it was smoking! Then she slammed the receiver down and sank back in her chair. What a morning! What a damn awful morning!

And the blood rushed out of her head. Leaping up, she felt the walls spin, the floor buck up to meet her. She fell to her knees, catching hold of the chair cushion and clinging there. *Jack!* It was past eleven and she hadn't gone to get him, hadn't even called! He'd think she had forgotten him. And she *had* forgotten!

Another wave of sickness washed over her. There was something wrong with her. Something was definitely the matter; something was missing or broken. Here was the most wonderful man in the world, the most handsome, the bravest, strongest, most exciting man, and she'd left him standing at the curb. Was she crazy?

Grabbing her shoulder bag, she raced out the door.

The hour-long drive to the hospital seemed to take ten hours.

He wasn't waiting outside, in front of the main entrance. "Obviously, you dope!" she muttered, "since it's ninety-five degrees and you're three hours late!" She zipped into a parking spot and ran up the drive to the main waiting room. No Jack. Up to the nurse's station on two. No Jack.

"Well, Abby, *there* you are," said Lorene Gray, the nurse who had delivered Jeanette sixteen years before. "Guess you and Mr. Gallagher got your wires crossed."

"Where is he?'"

"Why, Jeanette came and picked him up. When he couldn't reach you—"

"Business crisis," Abby interrupted, too flustered to maintain her usual reserve.

"That's what they figured." The nurse laughed. "Anyway, they're long gone." Picking up a chart, she added, "He's some looker, that fellow of yours."

"Pardon?" Abby stared.

"Now, Abigail Jean, I may be married thirty-seven years come October, but I still do notice things. And that one's hard to miss. They sure do raise 'em big in Colorado, don't they?" With a hearty laugh, she sailed into a patient's room.

Abby raised a cloud of dust along the dirt road to the marina. "Jack? Hello—hello—" she called, jumping onto the deck of the houseboat. "Jack?" She heard a crash and a clatter from inside, and then there he was in the doorway, a dark, tousled-haired giant, bare-chested, leaning on a pair of crutches.

"Well, hello."

"Hi." She was balanced on the edge of hysteria; she didn't know whether to laugh or cry. "Hi. Oh, you look fine." Her heart tumbled over. "Oh, Jack, I'm sorry. Things got crazy this morning just as I was going out the door to get you, and then I couldn't get away, and—and I'm sorry." The wave of momentum that had carried her this far crested and withdrew. "I'm sorry."

"It's okay. Come on in."

With the sun blocked by the awning, his face was in shadow, and she couldn't read his eyes. Was he angry? Was that a cool "come in"? Had he had it with her? Oh, she wouldn't blame him, but—

She followed him inside. As he pivoted to face her, one crutch caught on the near leg of the coffee table, sending a bowl flying. "Damn!" he cursed, batting at the table with the crutch tip.

"Oh, you *are* angry!"

"Of course I'm angry. I've been on these things one day, and already I've broken the night table, an umbrella stand, and that bowl! By the time I'm done, I'll own this boat! And I don't even like it! I feel like a caged cougar!"

"I'm sorry, Jack. Really—"

He stopped growling and looked at her, a wry grin tugging at the corners of his mouth. "And what are you sorry for? You didn't send me in after that alligator. Hey, you're the first good thing that's happened to me all day." Dropping one crutch with a bang, he reached out and touched her cheek. "Come here."

"Oh, Jack"—she leaned against his chest—"I feel so rotten. I wasn't there to get you this morning, and the other night . . . the other night I didn't tell you how much I love you."

"I noticed."

She pressed her face into his shirt so that the fabric muffled her words. "I—I really don't know what happened. I was just so mad at you, and so scared, it was like I wanted to punish you for making me feel all that. But if anything had happened to you—"

"Nothing happened. And nothing's going to happen."

"But it could. You keep doing all these wild, risky things, and something's bound to happen. I can't stand it. I really can't. I don't want to love you this much."

Jack let the other crutch clatter to the floor and wrapped his arms around her, leaning on her so that she had to hold some of his weight while he held her. "What *do* you want, Abby? You want to love me a little, enough to make you feel good, but not more? Not enough to hurt? Not enough to scare you? I don't know how to love that way."

He covered her mouth with his, kissing her fiercely. She couldn't breathe; his grip hurt her ribs. But when he drew his tongue and lips away, she clung to him, slipping the tip of her tongue into his mouth, across his smooth, firm lips. She nipped at his chin, kissed his cheek, rubbed her mouth against the raspy stubble of his beard.

"Forget what I said," she whispered. "I love you madly, I do."

"And I love you. But if I don't sit down, I'm going to fall down. Better yet, grab the other end of this coffee table."

Balancing with one arm, he grabbed the near side of the table, and together they hoisted it on top of the couch. Then Jack stretched out on the floor, pulling her down on top of him.

"Are you sure I won't hurt you?" she asked.

"You couldn't. Now, talk to me, girl."

Abby blushed. "Talking wasn't what I had in mind right now, Jack." And she nuzzled up against him, finding relief in the solid bulk of his body, its beauty and power. She wanted to climb right into his skin and hide there. Wrapping her arms around his neck, she pressed against him. "Hug me. Hug me so tight, I can't breathe. Jeanette says that makes everything all better, so hug me tight."

"What needs to be all better, Abby?"

"Nothing. Everything. Oh, I don't want to talk now. I only want you to hold me."

So he held her tight.

When he finally felt her relax, he whispered, "Abby, talk to me." Gently he separated the two of them, leaving one muscled arm as a pillow beneath her head.

"Well?" he prompted softly.

She felt so awkward, so transparent. With a little shrug she answered, "Mostly I felt terrible about these last few days. I'm so sorry they happened."

"Forgotten. What else?"

She squirmed in discomfort, pressing her face back into his shoulder. "Oh, it's too confusing to explain."

"Try me. Let me in, Abby, share it with me. You're always trying to keep everything in neat little compartments: Your family, your work, me. But life isn't neat. You'll go crazy trying, and you'll miss out on something good."

"What?" she whispered.

"Me. The love I can give. The help. The strength."

"But it isn't your problem."

"Make it mine!"

She rested her cheek on his arm and looked at him. "I'm afraid if I lean on you, I won't be able to stand on my own again. I'm afraid I'll need you and then you'll go away. I know you say you'll be back, but what if you get home, home to your mountains and your rivers, and that wildness grabs hold of you again? I can see the restlessness in you now. And what about Pop? Now you only miss him a little, because you know you're going back—but could you leave him? Could you? I couldn't," she whispered. "And I couldn't go with you, even if you asked me. But—but how could I stand it then? How could I live?"

"Oh, darlin'." He kissed her on the tip of her nose. "I do miss the mountains and the rivers. And I do love that old man—but I love you more. At least I think I do, and I'm willing to risk all the rest to find out. But I can't do it alone."

Abby pressed her face to his chest, hiding behind the curtain of her hair. "Gallagher," she began in a shaky little whisper, "sometimes you just steal my breath away. I mean, nothing in my whole life prepared me for you. I'm good at all the wrong things: I can put on a good front, I can pretend I don't need anyone's help—but I don't know how to do *this*. Nobody ever said things like this to me before."

"It's lucky, or I'd have to round 'em up and punch 'em in the nose." And, having made her laugh, he grabbed her wrists and rolled over on top of her. "Are you okay now?"

She nodded. "I do love you," she said, trapped as she was under his delicious weight. "I don't know why you want to be loved by a stubborn, short-tempered woman, but I'm yours."

"Good. Any other problems?"

"One. Simon. We had a really mean argument at the café, and now I've found out he's been making decisions behind my back. He made me look like a fool in front of the whole county!"

Jack's eyes flashed with fury, but he kept his voice steady. "Abby, no one would ever think that. You're the most determined, most courageous woman I've ever met, and all your friends and neighbors know it." He let that sink in, then added softly in a voice that made the hair rise at the back of her neck, "I'll take care of him. I'll straighten this out."

"Heavens, no! I told you, I've got to handle this myself, Jack. I have to *prove* I can."

"Prove it to whom, Abby?"

"To *me*, Jack. To myself."

"Don't be your own worst enemy, Abigail Jean."

"You be my best friend, okay, Gallagher? Keep reminding me that *this* is real. That life can be this wonderful, even when it gets this hard. Promise?" Her wide blue eyes begged for compliance.

Jack drew her face to his. Brushing his lips across hers, he said, "That's an easy promise to keep. Letting you struggle through this by your own stubborn self is the hard part."

"A test of your self-control, sir," she said, feeling whole again, safe. "Now"—she smiled—"I really have to get going. Roll off. I can't budge you and I can barely breathe."

"That's too bad," he murmured against her throat. "But I haven't got *that* much self-control!"

"Oh, *this* is called taking unfair advantage—!" She struggled to get her arms between them so she could push him off. "Jack! Ooomph . . ." She gave him a futile little shove, then collapsed. "Jack . . ."

He rolled off onto one hip, then propped his head up on one hand. "I must be crazy to let you get away now. You're damn hard to catch!"

Abby reluctantly stood up. "I'll try not to be so difficult."

"I'll believe that when I see it!"

She narrowed her eyes and put her hands on her hips. All the resolutions she had made in front of the mirror that morning came rushing back. "You think I can't change? I'll show you!" Laughing, she crouched down, pushed hard against his bare chest, and sent him sprawling on his back. "Gallagher, take me to the beach this weekend!"

Disbelief and desire warred in his dark eyes. "Are you sure?"

"Yes! Of course," she added, "we can't go till Sunday, and you'll have to get me back in time for the market on Monday, and you'll have to wait tables for me on Tuesday, but yes," she insisted, laughter bubbling through her words, "I sure do need a weekend with you at the beach. That is, if you're up to it."

"I'll manage." He grinned. "Thanks for the invite."

Ten

"Wherever we're heading, it had better take a good hour. Let me near the water now and I'd sink."

"No one told you to eat all those biscuits, Jack."

"It's not my fault your mother made great biscuits. And since you insisted we show up for Sunday breakfast, I figured I'd better make a good impression."

"Well, you certainly made an impression! An even dozen? Shame on you!"

Jack grinned, shifted the Jeep into first, and headed down the highway. "So, navigator, what's our destination?"

"Thought I'd take you to the Atlantic this time. Down near Cocoa Beach. Pretty beaches and nice surf—especially with this wind picking up."

"Cocoa? Hey, we can stop at that RonJon's surf shop your sister's always talking about."

"Jack, that's okay for kids."

"Don't be an old fuddy-duddy. I'll buy us some T-shirts and Jams and sunglasses, and we can be real tourists."

"Gallagher, you *are* a tourist! And a nut! Why don't you just give me the money, and I can invest it in a new juice squeezer for the Paradise."

"How exciting!"

"There's more to life than excitement."

"There's more to life than work."

"Here we go again!"

They both laughed. And when Abby shook her hair back in the wind and tossed him a smile, Jack breathed more easily, seeing that the shadows were fading from her blue eyes.

As he took the cutoff leading away from Titusville and the Cape, he craned his neck, searching for a glimpse of the shuttle on the launch pad. "Hey, one weekend let's head over to the space center. I've got to see a launch."

"Oh, you can see them from Orlando, even: the white contrail and the bright dot of the rocket. It's great."

"Not enough. I want to be so close, I can feel the roar. Feel the power. Feel the earth tremble."

"Here," she said, sliding her hand slowly up his thigh. "Feel the earth tremble."

Eyes flashing, he caught her hand between his knees and kept it trapped there.

Abby tried to tug it free. "Stop, Jack. You can't drive and play."

"You started it," he said. "But we can get back to that later. Can we drive and talk?"

"Sounds possible," she admitted, stealing a nervous glance at him out of the corner of her eye. "What do you want to talk about?"

"I got a call from Pop."

Her heart slipped down to her stomach. "Oh? Everything okay?"

"Basically okay. He got himself hurt a few days ago. He was digging for crystals in a small cave on a riverbank and caused a rockslide. Luckily he ended up with only a couple of bruised ribs and a bad ankle, but he says he found a beauty. Wrapped it in his shirt and drove himself to the hospital in Estes Park." Jack's chuckle was a mixture of admiration and frustration. "That old coot'll be the death of me yet!"

"But he is all right?"

"Says he's fine now. The wife of that couple taking care of the Lodge plied him with hot soup and hot compresses and kept a close eye on him. I'm glad she was there."

"But sorry you weren't."

"Yes," he answered softly, "of course I'm sorry. I wasn't there when he needed me, and he's always been there for me." He frowned and glanced out the window at the passing scrub palms and wetlands. "I'm going to have to go back, Abby. It worries me, with all the problems you're having right now, but I can't put it off much longer."

"Another week, Jack? If you could? I mean, I'm just trying out this new hug theory of Jeanette's"—she grinned self-consciously—"and I'd kind of hate to be alone right now."

He studied her carefully calm profile, her hands clasped, white-knuckled, in her lap. "All right," he said. He touched her hair. "All right."

Her face lit with a smile. "Okay! Then we are not going to talk about our worries this weekend. Not yours, and not mine. Please, Jack, let's not even *think* about them. I want to have a happy time, a fun, cozy, relaxing couple of days. That's what you promised."

"That's a promise I can keep. Now, why don't you direct us straight to RonJon's, darlin', and I don't want to hear a word of protest."

Sunlight glinted off the windshield, off the hood of the car, off the long ribbon of highway ahead. In the heat the light shimmered like water. The road eventually lifted in a shining arc over the Banana River, and in moments the ocean was there in front of them; ten shades of blue lay shining in the sun.

The "World's Largest Surf Shop" was a bright, splashy, flashy chaos. Surfboards, boogie boards, jet skis, and rafts hung from the ceilings and lined the aisles. You had to inch between them and the mob of shoppers all smelling of coconut oil and lotion and salt and sweat.

Before Abby knew what was happening, Jack had hefted a surfboard off its display and was being sold promises of the ultimate thrill by an eighteen-year-old in Ray-Bans and a flat top.

"No," she said with a gasp, hurrying over. "Do not sell this man a surfboard!"

Jack laughed. "He doesn't think I could learn in a day and a half, but I thought I'd give it a shot."

"No. Oh, Jack, please no. Remember your leg, the snake, the 'gator—" she begged, then changed tack faster than a sailor in a high wind. "Besides"—she fluttered her lashes and shifted into a sultry drawl—"I was hoping you'd have your hands full today, honey." Jack regarded her with amusement. Turning to the young man, he shrugged. "Next time. Thanks."

When he left, Abby rolled her eyes. "Oh, I can't *believe* I said that. The kid must think I'm going to jump your bones in the next aisle!" Her cheeks were pink.

"Well, you sure took his mind off surfboards! You even caught me by surprise."

"Desperation, Gallagher. Oh—the things you make me do!" She glared at him in mock ferocity. "I thought we were here to buy T-shirts."

So he bought her four T's decorated with sharks wearing sunglasses and flower leis, sharks surfing, and sharks skate-boarding.

"What am I going to do with all these?" she asked, laughing at him.

"Swim in them, sleep in them, I don't care! You look adorable."

"What about you?"

He held out a muscle shirt, and she could feel herself melt just imagining him in it. "I'm going to like that!" she said, grinning.

"That's what it's for." He grinned back.

Their motel was a five-story pink flamingo perched on the beach. In moments they had checked in, unpacked, and pulled on their swimsuits.

As Abby started to tug one of the new T-shirts over her head, she caught Jack's glance. He was watching her with that look of his—lips half-parted, eyes dark and eager—that meant he couldn't wait to get her in bed. Her heartbeat quickened. Her skin began to tingle. She could already feel his touch. "I know what you're thinking, Gallagher."

"Can't help it. You look so beautiful."

"This?" she said, fluffing the ruffle at the top of the suit. "It's an old, worn-out—" Her breath ran out, and she couldn't seem to draw another. Swallowing, she smiled, then bit her lip. "I knew I was going to be a sucker for that muscle shirt! Damn! Where *has* my willpower gone?"

"I don't know," he murmured against her lips, "but I hope it stays gone for good!"

When they finally got down to the beach, the sun was pinned straight up in the sky and the whole world seemed golden and dazzling. They rented wooden chaises with bright yellow cushions and a yellow umbrella that Jack speared into the sand and popped open immediately. Abby lay down in that welcome little oasis of shade and began applying sunscreen. "Do my back, would you?"

"Happily." His hands slid over the warm skin of her back, circling from her shoulders to the edge of her suit. "How about the back of your legs?"

"Umm . . . please."

"Anything else?"

"No, that's perfect!" She sighed contentedly. "I'm perfect and you're perfect, and this day's perfect, and I'm perfectly happy. This is just what I needed, Gallagher."

"Happy to oblige, darlin'."

The heat went to her brain like alcohol, pulling her down into a drugged half-sleep. The waves beat a constant refrain on the shore. The gulls circled overhead. She heard Jack's even breathing next to her, the rustle of pages as he read, the whisper of the breeze through his hair. Or did she dream it? Was this all a dream? The nearness of him? The sure, steady strength? The power of his body and the gentleness of his touch? Don't let me wake, she sighed in her dream. Don't let me wake. . . .

The first drop of water landed on her nose. Another on her chest. Then a cascade across her legs. With a yelp she was up and on her feet. "Gallagher, I'll get you for that," she said, gasping, but he ran into the water, laughing, spraying salt water in all directions. "Come on in," he yelled.

"No. I want to get good and hot first."

"You're hot enough. Come on!"

She started walking toward him with slow and teasing steps, but the sand was burning hot, and she ending up racing the last twenty yards and on into the surf. The water broke white and frothing across her thighs. She splashed on through the smaller breakers, following Jack. Then a big wave caught her across the chest and sent her reeling backward.

She stood back up, resisting the undertow and shaking sand from the lining of her suit. Jack was laughing at her. She could see that Tom Sawyer grin of his, his laughing eyes, his broad shoulders—and then the ocean lifted in a towering, white-crested wave above her, and she held her breath and dove right through it. The power of the wave swept along her body like a hand drawing over her, head to toe.

She surfaced laughing, shaking her golden hair back from her face. Jack waved, way out now, beckoning, and she swam to him with smooth, steady strokes.

Now they were past the point where the breakers crashed. She swam close and wrapped herself around his body. She rode him like a raft, resting on his chest, her legs locked around his hips. Leaning back, she spread her arms. Even through closed lids, she could see the sun; its brightness filled her head.

The ocean tugged at them, rising and falling. Salt dried on her face. When Jack reached behind her and lifted her back up into his arms, the kiss he gave her was salty. She ran her tongue over his lips.

"Let's swim awhile. I've got to stretch out these muscles," Jack said, and he lifted high and tossed her into the water.

He swam hard, paralleling the beach, and though she matched him stroke for stroke, she soon fell behind.

"Oh, what the heck!" She giggled. "That's too much like work." She rolled over onto her back and did a slow, lazy backstroke. One arm up, flutter kick, other arm up, kick, just a slow, lovely rhythm of movement through the cool, lovely water. Beads of water dropped from her arms across her face. Her cheeks felt hot and tight; behind her lids were sparkles of bright color.

She flipped over to her stomach, then pushed her head and shoulders under the water, feeling its coolness slide along her scalp. And with a kick she swam down, down, the water so clear, she could see the rocks on the bottom. Suddenly a quick, dark shape swam into view and Jack came up from below her, scaring the breath right out of her.

She broke the surface gasping and sputtering. "That's a helluva thing to do, Gallagher!" She pushed his dark head back under the water, feeling a rush of excitement after that split second of fear.

When he came to the surface she kissed his laughing mouth, their tongues and lips sliding over each other, her body wet inside and out. He must have known it, because he took hold of the ruffled edge of her suit and pulled it down, and the water was cold against her bare breasts but his mouth was hot, and she thought she would drown from the delicious dizziness of it all.

Instead she went wiggling away from him, laughing and splashing at him, keeping him at bay with one hand while she tugged her suit back up with the other. "Gallagher! You're awful! There are people around!"

"No one near by but us minnows."

"Ha! Shark is more like it— Oh, Lord, you made me say that word out here. Oh, you are the worst!" She did a three-hundred-sixty-degree turn, scanning the rippling surface of the water. "I'm getting out while the going is good. Jack, come with me," she called, already swimming toward shore. "It's not safe to swim alone."

"I'll be in."

"Gallagher!" She sputtered, overcome with exasperation. "Now!"

One dark brow lifted. His mouth curved in an amused smile. "I'll be in." He was treading water, his powerful arms circling shoulder high.

"Oooooh . . ." Muttering furiously to herself, Abby swam toward shore. She caught the crest of a good-size wave and rode it in, but the next came crashing down on top of her before she could get her footing, and she went rolling under, collecting sand in the most annoying places. She scrambled to her feet, dug in against the undertow, and then used the push of the next wave to propel her to the beach. Hands on knees, hair dripping in her eyes, she looked back out to sea.

She saw his dark head, the wave of one arm, and then he caught the crest of a huge wave and body-surfed it in to shore. Striding against the undertow, he reached her side.

"Not the Colorado, but it's not bad!" He shook sea spray in a wide arc and smiled down at her. "See how tame I'm getting? One word and here I am, darlin'."

"Impossible!" she muttered, and walked back down toward the surf.

"Where are you going now, woman?"

"To get the sand out of my suit! You, of course, have no such problems! Men!"

They built a sand castle with cups and plastic spoons. Three little boys came over to join in, bringing "professional" tools: plastic pails and shovels. When it was all finished, they built a moat with a canal running to the surf, and cheered when the sea filled it up. Then they walked miles along the beach, holding hands, bumping their hips together and laughing. As the wind picked up, Abby had to hang on to her wide, floppy beach hat.

"You still under there?" Jack asked teasingly, bending down to kiss her freckled nose. That pale, delicate nose, with its sprinkling of freckles, held some strange power over him. One look at her on a day like that one and it was as if someone had taken a sandbag and hit him smack in the stomach. He wanted to lift her in his arms, carry her away, never let her go.

The question was, would she ever let him? Would she ever trust him, admit that she needed him, that much? He gave her hand a quick, hard squeeze and kept on walking.

By four in the afternoon the wind was strong enough to tip over their umbrella. Abby shaded her eyes with the flat of one hand while Jack chased and caught the umbrella, then stowed it beneath his chair.

"Look at that." Abby pointed out to the horizon. There, where the sky met the sea, was a black line of clouds. "Big storm out there," she murmured. Then, looking up, she smiled. "How about treating this lady to a good cold drink at the pool bar?"

"Love to," Jack answered.

They gathered up their towels and lotion and paperback books and took the wooden boardwalk up to the deck.

The bar was a thatched-roof affair, four countertops surrounding one tattooed, slow-moving bartender. "What'll it be, folks?" she asked, sliding her eyes up and down Jack in open admiration.

"Longneck Bud for me. Abby?"

"A piña colada, please," Abby said, biting back an urge to laugh.

Her drink was plopped unceremoniously in front of her. Jack's was delivered so neatly, the woman had time to brush her fingers against his as she set the bottle down. "Longneck for you, handsome."

Abby felt the giggles bubbling in her throat like soda-pop fizz. Giving up, she hid behind a napkin, coughing fiercely while she grabbed her drink and swung round on her barstool. Jack cupped his hand around her elbow and led her to a distant chaise longue.

"Thought that was funny, huh, sweet thing?"

"Longneck for you, handsome," she drawled, giggling again. Then she tipped her head to one side, her spell of silliness disappearing. "Sometimes I think these days with you are a dream, Gallagher. It's so wonderful to be happy. I just wish I could figure out how to feel like this all the time, how to tie all the parts of my life together. Most of the time I feel I'm being torn in ten different directions. There's my parents, and Jeanette, and money and bills and the Paradise, and now Simon. Sometimes I just don't know what to do."

"I understand, Abby. But maybe you try to do too much. Maybe you ask too much of yourself—"

"And how much is *too* much?" she asked. "It all depends on me. It's my responsibility!"

"Why does it all have to be yours? Sure, help your family—you're lucky to have them; they're lucky to have you—but do they have to be the center of your life? Same with the business—"

"Oh, you'll never understand! Forget it. Just forget I said anything."

"I can't forget it, Abby," he said with a growl. "It's always there between us."

"What a nasty thing to say!" she snapped, turning away. She took a swallow of her drink and licked her lips. When she looked back, his demanding eyes were still on her.

She met his gaze with her own stubborn stare. "Sometimes you make me feel so pressured. Like I'm not—not—" She frowned, feeling guilty and defensive and angry all at the same time. "Like I'm not giving enough, or something!"

"That's not at all what I mean."

"Then what? You think I'm too committed to my restaurant, my parents, my sister?"

"No," he insisted with that same maddening control. "I just wonder if you've decided where I fit into all that."

Her eyes widened. "Right in the middle! Right at the heart of everything." With sudden shyness she reached out and touched his arm. "Don't you believe me?"

"I want to." He stood up. A strange, almost vulnerable look came into his eyes, and then he turned away and walked over to the deck railing.

Abby jumped up, spilling her drink all over the table. "Jack!" She ran and grabbed his arm. "Jack, don't be mad at me. Please!"

"Hey, I'm no kid." He towered over her, frowning and dark. "I'm not 'mad at' you, as you put it. Abby, I'm thirty-five years old, and before I met you, I was happy with my life. Happy alone with my rivers and mountains. But now I love you; I'll love you forever. You've taken over the center of me, and I stay here waiting to see if I'm *your* center." His eyes seemed to bore deep into her. "But I still don't know, and, darlin', despite all the lovin', I don't think you know yourself."

Jack leaned back against the railing, his arms crossed over his chest. "I've never been very good at waiting. And, woman, you've given me more practice in this short time with you than I've had in all my years."

"I know," she whispered. "And I'm sorry."

"You don't have to apologize. But sometime soon you're going to have to do something much more difficult: You're going to have to decide. I've put everything else on hold—but it can't stay that way forever." His gaze was silent, powerful. And then it was as if he took hold of himself and stepped back to give her space. His eyes softened, and he smiled. "But it's not this minute. Right now you look like a little fried clam."

"How romantic." Her eyes filled with grateful tears at his teasing. "Maybe I'll go up and hop in the shower and come out gorgeous—and I'll make up for being such a crazy lady! What d'ya think?"

Jack nodded, tipped her chin up, and kissed her fiercely on the mouth. "Go ahead. I'll be up soon."

"Now, stay away from my competition, Gallagher!" She forced a smile and rolled her eyes toward the bar.

"I'll try," he said, returning her smile.

Abby fell back against the elevator wall, fanning her face with the brim of her hat, keeping her mind carefully empty. *An aspirin! My kingdom for an aspirin*, she thought. When the door slid open, she clattered down the hall to their room. Two aspirin later, she wrapped herself in her robe, tossed the wet things on the chairs out on the balcony, and flopped down across the bed. *Now, if I just nap for ten minutes, everything will be okay. . . .* She closed her eyes.

A constant, loud tap-tapping woke her. "Ohhh," she groaned, sitting up and trying to get her eyes to focus. "Jack?" she called, and hurried to the door. No one was there. Puzzled, she glanced down at her watch. "Six o'clock!" She frowned. "Goodness, I really fell asleep," she said to the empty room. And then the tap-tapping came again, and she realized it was coming from out on the balcony. Had Jack come up while she slept?

Crossing the room, she yanked the curtains back. The wet end of one towel slapped against the window. Abby smiled. "Chicken!" she said aloud.

She slid the glass door open, and the wind filled the room. It lifted the drapes and pushed her robe against her legs. The sky was growing dark with storm clouds, black shapes galloping in over the beach, their edges illuminated by the eerie play of lightning on them. It wasn't raining there yet, but out over the ocean she could see the streaked gray curtain of the rain.

And then her eye was drawn to a lone figure on the empty beach. "Jack!" she shouted, but her voice was blown back in her face.

After pulling on shorts and a T-shirt, she rode the elevator down and ran out toward the beach. The wind blew her hair in her eyes, but she raced along the boardwalk and down onto the sand.

When she saw him, a strange feeling of fear enveloped her.

Jack was standing at the ragged edge of the surf. His feet and legs were buried in wet sand up to his calf muscles, so she knew he had been standing there a long time, not moving, simply looking out to sea. The towering clouds, black as night, reached up from the horizon to the top of heaven.

The surf was coming in strong, crashing against him, so that she could see the muscles tighten across his thighs as the waves smashed into him. She could see him jolted back, yielding, and recovering his balance, waiting for the next onslaught.

What was the man doing?

That unnamed fear reached down to her heart.

"Hi!" she yelled. "Jack! Jack!" She ran to him, kicking up sand that blew back to sting her legs and face. "Jack, hi!" She grabbed his arm, swung his torso around. "Hey, what are you doing, Gallagher?"

Jerked from his thoughts, Jack looked down at her, smiled gently, and pulled her snugly against his side. He looked back out to sea. "I really miss it," he answered.

Abby gave a frantic little laugh. "You mean we don't have enough water for you in Florida?"

"You know what I mean, Abby." Kicking his legs free, he turned and wrapped her in his arms. He stared over her head at the gathering storm. "This is the way I like things, with a bite to them! Trouble is," he whispered, rubbing his chin against her hair, "where I come from, nature had the bite but my women were soft. Down here, damned if I haven't run into the opposite!"

"You're going to leave me, aren't you?" she cried. She locked her arms around his waist and clung to him. "You're going to go back."

Prying her loose, he looked down at her face. "I've got to return. I have a business to run, too, and I need to help with the lodge. Besides, I want to see it all again. I miss it. I miss the power, the excitement, the beauty of it all. I miss Pop and the lodge and the sheer cliffs and the wild valleys. I'm tired of sand. Tired of the heat and the bugs and the air conditioning. I've got to feel the cool wind off the mountaintops—"

"But you won't come back! You'll forget me—or get yourself killed on some river!"

"Preferably the latter?" He grinned and brushed his hand over her cheek.

"Don't laugh at me, Gallagher!"

"How can I help it, when you're funny? I told you I love you—"

"But that isn't always enough."

"How do you know, Abby? You've never given it a chance."

People were starting to gather in the lobby, and when Jack pulled the door open and the wind whipped in, their voices rose to a new level of excitement. Abby caught the words *hurricane* and *Bahamas* as she held tightly to Jack's waist on their way to the elevator.

She wanted to be allowed to hold tightly to him without having to explain or offer anything. *What a foolish, selfish person I'm becoming!* she thought. She couldn't find a thing to say the whole, silent ride up. She just held on.

When they got to their door, Jack hugged her to him. "Relax, Abby. You've got yourself all strung out. You know, some old river rat once said you've got to go easy over the rough spots. Just ride 'em out, darlin'."

Abby slumped against his shoulder. "Is that some old river rat I know?"

"Intimately."

Inside they flipped on the TV. Sure enough, the weatherman was tracing the route of the season's first hurricane on its wild way to the islands. Three days of solid rain were guaranteed for south and central Florida.

"Jack, I'm just going to call home and make sure everything's okay," Abby said, reaching for the phone.

"Good. Then I get the shower." Jack pulled the

muscle shirt over his head and stepped out of his trunks. Naked, he walked around the room, looking for his deodorant and after-shave. Abby misdialed. His body was so beautiful, so amazing and powerful. He sat down on the bed next to her, watching the news, and her heart filled with a bittersweet desire at the touch of his bare hip. Abby dialed again, and the phone rang once, twice. She lightly touched his shoulder, and he turned and kissed her neck. "Oh, Jack," she breathed, "I do love you— Hi, Jeanette!" she said loudly.

Jack rose and went into the bathroom.

"Jeanette, how's everything? . . . What? It's me, Abby. Who do you think is is? . . . Very funny, Jeanette."

When Jack stepped out of the shower, Abby was leaning against the vanity, waiting for him.

"That's a surprise!" Jack said. "But you could have come on in. I'm very informal in the shower."

"Jack, I've got to ask a favor."

Jack shook his head, his face clouding like the sky outside. "Don't tell me. You want to go home."

"Please, Jack. Simon's been calling all day—he says he's got to talk to me *immediately*. I can't even imagine what he's up to now, but Jeanette says he sounds even stranger than usual and—"

"Can it wait till morning, at least?"

"But it's going to rain anyway, and we won't get back down on the beach—"

"I wasn't worried about the beach." He stepped close, resting his hands on the vanity top on either side of her, so that his hard, wet body pressed against hers. "Sometimes you are really dense, my darling."

She blushed. "I know." Then she looked up at him beseechingly. "Jack, I know it's a lot to ask."

"You're damn right it is." He bit back the rest of his words. "Okay, pack your bag. I'll go down and pay the bill."

•　　•　　•

They drove through steady rain from Cocoa to Orlando. North of the city, the sky was threatening, but the rain held off.

"So, where am I taking you?" Jack asked shortly. "Your place or the restaurant?"

"To the Paradise. I left a message with Jeanette that Simon could meet me there around ten. And if he's not there"—she shrugged, offering a hopeful smile—"well, then it can't be so important, and we can go to my place and I'll make you something to eat. Okay?"

"Dandy."

Two cars were parked in the café's lot, Simon's and another.

"You don't think it's those thugs from Miami again, do you?" Abby asked, trying to peer into the other car's lit interior.

"It's a different car, different plates, but we'll soon find out. You wait here. Keys are in the ignition; just get going if there's any trouble." He stepped out and headed toward Simon's car.

Simon met him halfway, smiling and waving to whomever was in the other car. The doors opened, and sure enough, two men stepped out, but they were pleasant-looking men, middle-aged and dressed in suits.

Jack glared at Simon's weasel face. "This better have been important."

"Oh, it's important, all right." He pointed toward Abby. "So, is she coming out or are we going to hold this meeting in the parking lot?"

"I'd like to shove your face in this parking lot," Jack said, his voice low and menacing.

Simon took a hasty step back.

Jack turned to the other two. "This couldn't have waited until tomorrow?"

The two men looked at each other, surprise and

nervousness clearly written on their faces. "Well, Simon said he was leaving town tomorrow, and insisted we—I mean, he said that Ms. Clarke suggested we meet tonight. Is something wrong?"

The muscles tightened in Jack's jaw. "There'd better not be. Wait here."

He turned and strode back to the car. "Abby, come on out. Whoever these guys are, they're not dangerous."

Abby said a quick hello as she walked by them, then unlocked the door of the café. All five of them stepped into the dining room. "Why don't you have a seat?" she said, and sank into a chair. She looked expectantly from one person to another, then focused on Simon. "Well, what's so important?"

"I sold my half of the restaurant to these guys, and they want to buy you out," Simon said, leaning his chair back on two legs.

Jack grabbed his shoulder and pulled him back down with a thump that made his teeth rattle. "You did what?"

"I sold my half. I'm allowed to." His voice was a whine. "It's perfectly legal. These guys had it written up by a lawyer. I've got my money. It's all done!"

Abby stood up, her eyes so wide, the whites showed all around. "But how could you do that? This is my restaurant. I love this place, and I have no intention of selling it. Not to anybody! Do you all understand that?"

Both men rose hastily. "Ms. Clarke, we were led to believe that you'd be interested in selling—at the right price, of course."

"Well, that's a lie. That's a damn lie! And you can't make me. You *can't* force me out—"

"Take it easy, Abby," Jack whispered, slipping an arm around her shoulders.

She pulled away, shouting, "You can't make me sell. If you try I'll fight you. I'll go to court. I'll—I don't know *what* I'll do, but—" She started to shake, and her voice broke.

"Please, Ms. Clarke," said one of the men. "Please don't upset yourself. Take it easy."

"Yeah, take it easy." Simon rose with a nasty laugh. "Gee, you've turned into a nervous bitch."

Abby gasped.

Jack put his hands on her shoulders and moved her to one side. Then he smashed Simon in the jaw. Simon went down like a sack of potatoes.

The taller of the two men looked from Simon, on the floor, up to Jack. "Bet he never even saw that coming."

"He should have," his partner answered. "Anyway, he's bound to remember it for a good long while. What did Simon say your name is?"

"He didn't. It's Jack Gallagher."

"Well, Mr. Gallagher, we'll be sure to remember that. Now, we're not looking for trouble. This is strictly business."

"Fine. Then why don't you gentlemen have your lawyer put this purchase offer down on paper, with an appropriate buy-out clause, and get back to Ms. Clarke's lawyer."

"Fine. Whom do we have it sent to?"

"It—it's on the partnership agreement," Abby said, fighting to hide her trembling. "I'm sure you have a copy of that."

"We certainly do. Thank you. And have a nice evening."

Eleven

"What time is it?"

"You just asked me that, Abby. It's still only three o'clock in the morning, and no, you can't call your lawyer now."

"But I've got to warn him about those men! I've got to get him started on some kind of a counterattack."

"Not at three A.M.," Jack repeated, shifting his weary frame on her narrow couch. "Can we go to bed now?"

"You go ahead. I couldn't sleep." She paced back and forth in front of him, wringing her hands. "Oh, my head is pounding." She rubbed one hand over her cheek. "Even my teeth hurt."

Jack rose and put his arms around her. "Let me give you a back rub—"

She jerked away, annoyance written all over her face. "That's not what I need now."

"Fine." He shoved his hands in the pockets of his jeans. "Abby, don't make more out of this than it is."

She swung on him. "Oh, this isn't enough? I guess it just doesn't compare with riding some dumb rubber raft down some dumb river."

Jack stared at her. Then he drew a slow breath through clenched teeth. "Abby, until they send you a copy of the legal papers, you don't even know what you're faced with—"

"I'm faced with losing the Paradise!" she wailed.

"They can't just force you out."

"Can't they? How the hell do you know? You don't know anything about this!" She picked at a cuticle until it bled, then stuck her finger in her mouth. She felt wild now, reckless with anger. "Oh, it's too bad a bear didn't attack the café, or a raft overturn in my parking lot. Then you could be a *real* expert! But now you just don't know anything about it, do you?" She spit the words at him and swung across the room.

Jack grabbed her arm and yanked her back, but at her first gasp of dismay he let go. "I'm sorry." His face had gone white. "Sorry." He backed away, hands spread, breathing hard. "I know you're scared, and if you need someone to take it out on—"

"Oh, what a brave and noble soul!" she snapped.

Jack's body grew rigid. "Why the hell are you mad at me, Abby?"

"Because if you hadn't been here, I'd have been paying attention. I would have seen what Simon was up to. I'd have stayed one step ahead—"

"Bullshit. You chose a bad partner, and he's pulled a fast one."

"Oooh!" Her breath popped out in an explosion of anger. "So it's my own fault? *My* ineptitude? *My* stupidity?"

"That's not what I meant, dammit—"

"That's what you said. It's what *everyone's* going to say! All these years, all this hard work, and I'm going to fail in front of *everyone*! But maybe you and everybody else expected it, and I'm the only one who's surprised!" She shoved at him with all her might. "Just leave me alone! Go away!"

"Abby"—he held her tightly, letting her struggle

vainly against him—"Abby, don't hurt yourself over this. It'll be okay. It'll work out. And, darlin', it's only a business, only a restaurant—"

"No!" she cried. "It's all I have!"

Jack's head snapped back as if she had hit him. "Really? Then what the *hell* am I doing here?"

Turning on his heel, he slammed out the door and strode away, carrying his silent fury into the dark night.

She took three aspirin and refused to think. It didn't matter. Nothing mattered. She would just wait, wait until morning, and then she could call the lawyer and he'd help her and everything would be okay again, and then Jack would come back, he'd surely come back, he'd know she hadn't meant any of it. But she wouldn't think about it till morning.

Jack did come back. At ten the next morning, he knocked twice, loudly, then let himself in. He found her sprawled on the couch, still wearing the wet raincoat she had worn to the lawyer's office earlier.

"Abby?" he whispered, kneeling beside her. His eyes were dark as bruises in his drawn face, but they softened at the sight of her. "Sweet thing? Hey, you crazy kid, you're soaking wet."

He untied her belt and pulled the coat down off her shoulders and tossed it in the corner.

She grumbled in her sleep, her exhausted body fighting to hold on to this sweet escape. *Don't let me wake, don't let me wake. . . .* But with the thought, she was awake. Her eyes fluttered open, dazed and unfocused.

"Hello, Abby. You okay?"

"Jack?" She sighed, resting her cheek on one hand. She stared at him myopically, without the slightest trace of recognition.

"Just wait here. I'll get you some coffee."

He brought back a steaming mug and waited silently while she sipped it. Then he lumbered to his feet. "Come on. You've got to get out of those wet clothes."

She looked down at herself in surprise. "Oh. I'm all wet." Puzzlement creased her brow. Then, lifting one finger, she nodded. "I remember. It was pouring. I went to the lawyer's office, and it was pouring, and I had to wait in the hall. . . . But didn't I have a raincoat? I thought—"

"It's over there." He pointed, already leading her toward the bedroom.

"Good. Thought maybe I'd lost my marbles."

He gave a short, harsh bark of a laugh, handed her a towel, and pulled a robe from her closet. "There. Get dry."

She stopped and looked up at him with a crooked little smile. "Haven't you got an old sweat shirt around, mister?"

A look of pain flashed across his face as he turned away.

Abby looked confused. "I was just—I mean, it reminded me of that first time—"

"I *know* what you were remembering!" His brusqueness made her flinch, but before she could say a word, he had her in his arms. "Oh, God, woman. I love you so much." He breathed in the damp smell of her hair, then pushed her gently away. "Get dressed. I'll wait out there."

She came out brushing her limp hair, the sleeve of her robe falling away from her pale arm. She looked so fragile that his heart ached, but he knew her too well to baby her. "Okay, tell me what your lawyer said."

She shrugged and sat down on the edge of one chair. The brush lay forgotten in her lap. "He said he would contact their lawyers today, but that most likely Simon's sale to them was legal, and that they would have every right to make a buy-out offer." Her shoulders sagged. "He said that once we get a copy of the papers, we can 'study the facts, examine the options—several courses will be open to us.' He said he'd be in touch." She gave an unconvincing little laugh.

Jack reached over, took both her hands in his, and pulled her onto his lap. She ignored the hairbrush as it fell to the floor. "I wish I could make it all better."

"So do I." She sighed and let her head fall against his shoulder. "Right now I'm not feeling so good."

Jack brushed his lips across the top of her head.

At his touch, Abby reached up and wrapped her arms around his neck. "Jack—I'm sorry about last night."

"I'll get over it."

She looked up at him. "But you haven't yet?"

"Not quite." He gave her a wry smile. "But I'll live. Anyway, what do you do next?"

"That's the worst thing!" she said, standing up. "I can't go out and *do* anything. I've got to wait. Mark time at the café as if it were business as usual, and wait! Wait for their lawyer's papers, wait for my lawyer's suggestions, wait for their lawyer's response. Oh"—she tossed her head—"damn! I think I'll go crazy!"

She kicked the brush and started to pace again.

Jack stood and grabbed hold of her. "Enough of that. It's Monday, and we're going to the farmers' market. You've got ten minutes to get ready. Go!"

Bleary-eyed, Abby obeyed.

When the phone rang, she was stepping out of the shower. "I'm coming, I'm coming! Jack, I'll get it!" she yelled, flashing by in a towel. "Maybe it's my lawyer. Maybe—" She grabbed the phone, her face flushed. "Yes, hello?"

There was a tiny pause. She looked down at the

receiver in surprise and then held it out stiffly to Jack. "It's for you. It's a woman."

Frowning, Jack took the phone. "Hello? Gallagher here." He listened in silence. Less than a minute passed, but it was enough time for the blood to drain from his face, leaving his lips white-edged.

Abby started to move closer, but the look in his eyes held her at bay.

When he did speak, his chest heaved and the breath rasped in his throat. "Okay," he said, "I'll be right there. . . . Yes, I understand. . . . I said, yes, dammit! Now, hang up so I can call the airlines."

He pressed the disconnect button and stood holding the receiver to his chest, his dark eyes sightless.

"Jack . . . ?"

His voice came from far away. "It's Pop. He's back in the hospital with internal bleeding. Something they didn't catch the other day . . . He—" Jaw clenched tight, he shook his head and tried again. "He—oh, Lord . . ." The pain in his face was terrible to see.

Abby tried to touch him. "Jack?"

"Get me the phone book! Hurry, we've got to get a flight out now."

"Jack, I'm so sorry. What—?"

"Hurry! We've got to get there. We've got to get there *now*, you understand? He's all the family I've got—" His voice broke.

"Here," she whispered, "let me dial for you."

"No. Just go throw some things in a suitcase. Where the hell is 'airlines'? There!" He stabbed at the numbers, then leaned heavily against the wall. "Answer . . . answer, already!" The sweat stood out on his brow and stained dark circles under his arms. "Answer, already, will you! . . . Hello! Yes, I need to make a reservation on your next flight out to Denver . . ." He was breathing like a boxer taking a beating. "What? Hang on." He turned to Abby. "Can we make a twelve-thirty?"

She glanced at her watch and shook her head.

"Damn!" Spearing his fingers through his hair, he grabbed hold and yanked, hard. "No. What's your next one? . . . Well, who else flies out there? . . . Do *they* have a flight in between— Listen, would you *help* me with this, lady? This is an emergency! . . . Yes." He closed his eyes. "Yes, we'll take that. . . . Why *can't* you make the reservation? . . . Okay, give me the number. Thanks."

He hit the disconnect button and started redialing. His eyes sought Abby's face and rested there, as if only the sight of her held off his panic.

Nothing had ever frightened Abby so much as the look of him, wild and grieving.

"Go pack." He nodded toward the bedroom, then jerked his attention back to the phone. "Hello, I need two tickets on your flight 101, Orlando to Denver, and a rental car on up to Estes Park—today! . . ." He glanced at Abby, frowned, and mouthed the words *Go pack.*

Abby just stood there, suddenly unable to breathe.

Jack's face became still as stone. He stared at her, taking her measure—and his own. The he took a deep breath.

"It's okay, Abby. I understand."

"Jack"—she was gasping, desperate to explain—"I can't go now. I can't. The café, the lawyers . . ."

"I understand." Pain was etched in the lines of his face. Pain and betrayal. But he set his mouth, tightened his jaw, and pulled himself together. He wouldn't ask for more than she could give. And if he'd hoped for more, needed more, that was his own damn problem! "It's all right, Abby. I'll go alone."

Then he spoke into the phone. "Yes, I'm still here. I need one seat on that flight. . . . Gallagher. Jack . . . Yeah, thanks."

He reached for the phone book, knocked it to the floor, and bent to pick it up.

Abbey watched him, mute and frightened.

He flipped through the pages, his hands shaking. Found a number. Dialed.

"I need a cab to the Orlando airport, right now."

"Jack," she said, fighting for breath, "I'll take you."

"No," he said, his voice harsh with control. "No, not a good idea. You'd better stay by the phone. And I'd better get going."

With that same frightening control, he drew a hand slowly down her cheek. "I'll be back when I can."

Abby put her hand over his. "Let me drive you to the airport, Jack. Please . . ."

"No, darlin'. Right now, halfway won't help either of us."

Twelve

Where else would she go but the Paradise Café? She drove over, unlocked the back door, and stepped into the kitchen. Things were just as she'd left them. This was her place. This was what mattered. Right? Oh, wrong, wrong, wrong! All of a sudden, it was just a room. Just a kitchen in a nice little restaurant in a nice little town in central Florida. That was all it was. She blinked. And it was as if she were waking up from a dream she had fallen into years ago, in a high-school library, a dream about escaping poverty and fear. She had tumbled into that dream a desperate teenager—and not woken up till just this moment. Now it was love, and not fear, that filled her heart.

Jack! He was what mattered. He was the center of her life. He was everything!

Who else would she call but her family? When her mother answered the phone, Abby told her to hurry over, with all of them. She needed their help. There and then.

When they showed up, she wrapped them all in great big, unexpected hugs, scaring the heck out of them, so that they sank into their chairs, worried and wide-eyed. "Has something happened?" Jeanette asked, the only one able to find a voice.

"Chaos!" Abby assured her. "Simon's sold half the restaurant out from under me, and I don't know if I'll be able to fend off the buy-out. Pop's sick and in the hospital. And Jack's flown back to Colorado."

"And you didn't go with him?" It was her mother, startling them both.

Abby shook her head with a baleful grin. "Sometimes I'm not as smart as I think, Mom. And too stubborn to ask—"

"Or listen!" Jeanette chimed in, then threw an arm around her sister's shoulders. "'Or maybe just too busy taking care of all of us. So now tell us how we can help. We can. And we want to."

"Thanks, you all," she whispered.

And then, like a small whirlwind, she flew around the café, putting them all to work. She showed her father the reservation book and how to seat customers, at which tables and in which order. She told him what time to show up, and to wear his one dark suit. Then she stationed her mother at the phone with the week's orders and a message pad. "And if my lawyer calls, tell him I'll get back to him as soon as possible. After all, Mom, it *is* just a business, not my whole life." And then she sent Jeanette off to the farmers' market. "Fresh! I want everything fresh— just like you!" And she called Lena and Archie and asked them if they would do the cooking for the rest of the week and deal with the other help. "And pick the specials and give 'em your own touch! Thanks, y'all."

And then she left it in those capable, loving hands and raced home.

Threw a few things in a suitcase.

Called the airlines.

There was just one flight left that day to Denver, and she grabbed the last seat on it, congratulating herself all the way to the airport.

It was a center seat, and she sat squashed between a businessman and a mother with a baby, thinking about Jack and filled with this unnameable, uncontainable excitement.

Of course, nothing went according to plan. Nothing ever does.

The plane taxied out toward the runway, then taxied back with a "small mechanical failure." The cabin grew hot and noisy. The businessman grumbled; the baby screamed. Abby broke out in a cold sweat. Jack would have landed already. Would he go to the lodge? To the hospital? What hospital? Was Pop all right? *Oh, please, let him be all right, and let Jack be there in time! And please, if You could spare a minute, could we take off soon?*

They finally did take off, but an hour late, and she missed her connecting flight, and spent the night in a hard plastic seat in the Dallas–Fort Worth Airport.

The first flight in the morning was booked solid, but she was on the next, before noon, headed for Denver, her hair standing on end, her eyes bloodshot, her jeans and shirt pasted to her aching body.

In Denver she rented a car and sped up the highway, comforted by the mountains looming on the left, as close and real as Jack soon would be. *Jack.* "Oh, Jack, I'm coming," she whispered, looking out at those mountains. "I'm coming. Wait for me. Want me. Love me."

She drove once through Estes Park, scanning the unfamiliar streets, searching for the hospital. She felt her nerves fraying, her heart racing. She pulled into a coffee shop and got directions and a cup of black coffee.

The hospital was just blocks away, and she parked, then raced inside to the nurses' station. "Mr. Stout, please. It's important. Oh, please, let me see him for just a second. I'm a friend, and I've come all the way from Florida—"

"Take it easy, ma'am. It's all right. Mr. Stout's in

two-seventeen, and I'm sure he'll be glad to have some more company."

Swaying unsteadily, Abby grabbed hold of the counter top. "You mean he's okay? He's here, and I can see him? Really?"

"Yes, of course." The nurse slipped her arm around Abby's shoulder. "Now, you see, you shouldn't expect the worst."

"Old habit I'm trying to break," Abby said, giving a weak little smile. "Two-seventeen, you said?"

"Left off the elevator. Have a nice visit, dear."

"Thanks. Thanks so much." And then she was upstairs, at the door—a quick knock, and inside.

"Mr. Stout? Pop? Can I come in?"

"Well, I'll be!" The old man strained to lift his head, then waved her in with a hand frail as tissue paper. "Abby Clarke. Now, *that's* a nice surprise."

"Oh, Pop," she whispered with a catch in her throat, "I'm sorry it took me so long. Are you all right?"

"I'll be fine, little gal. Poked a rib into a lung and scared a lot of folks, me included, but I'm gonna be fine. Stop your worryin'; I've still got things to do and places to see." He cocked his head and gave her a quick once-over. "Now, I don't know what to make of this, but my visitors are looking a lot worse than I am. Know what I mean?"

"Maybe," she answered, dropping her eyes.

"Well, just maybe Jack was here yesterday and this morning, and he looked like hell. Finally had to send him away—he was making me so nervous! And now you, you're making me nervous too! So now that you know I'm a crotchety old man who's gonna last awhile yet, I'm gonna chase you on out of here also."

"Where should I go?" Abby asked, meeting his eyes.

The old man grinned. "Well, that's up to you, now, isn't it? But if you're interested, I sent Jack out to find a river. Seemed like the only safe place for him."

"A river? Oh no, not again." Then she straightened her shoulders. "Which river, Pop?"

"You'll have to ask Bear."

"Oh," She sighed, remembering their one and only meeting. "Bear, huh?"

" 'Fraid so. Guess nothing's easy, is it, little gal?" He patted her hand.

She gave his a good squeeze back. "Guess not," she said. "But I'm tough. Been tough all my life, when I only thought I knew what I wanted. Now that I'm sure, nothing can stop me!"

"Go get 'em!" the old man said, and laughed. When she vanished out the door, he smiled to himself. "What a pair!"

She drove into town, cruising the main street, reading the signs above the doors until she found what she was looking for: G & D White Water Rafting.

She parked out front and walked in. The room was filled with river rats and tourists, and Abby edged past them all to the wooden counter. She recognized Bear Dempsey before he recognized her. But when he did, he just stared coolly at her.

"Hello, Bear," she said, laying both hands flat on the counter. "I'm looking for Jack."

"He's not here."

"I know. He's out on a river somewhere. Which one?"

"Not sure." Eyes dark and flat, he turned to wait on the next customer.

She grabbed the front of his shirt, surprising herself as much as him. "Yes, you are, and you're going to tell me or I'm going to stand here and make such a fuss, I'll empty this room faster than you can say spit!"

"Nervy for a little bit of a thing, aren't you?" he said, staring down at the small hand hanging onto his shirt.

"Desperate."

"That so?" he rumbled, weighing the situation.

"Well, someone else I know went off looking desperate. But Jack's my friend. How do I know this is what he wants?"

Suddenly her voice shook. "Bear, *I* honestly don't know if it's what he wants anymore. But I want it. I've *got* to try, and *you've* got to help me. Please."

He looked at her, studying her the way he might a river or the sky, looking for signs, for clues. Then he nodded. "Okay. Get in the Jeep."

They drove southwest, up into the mountains.

"Where are we headed?" Abby asked, hanging onto the side of the Jeep, trying to match her bouncing to the bumps as the earth flew by.

"Boulder Creek. Still some decent water this time of year."

She swallowed hard. "I'll bet."

When they got there, a group of rafters was gathered in the bright sun near the water's edge, downing a few beers before the next run. Jack wasn't there.

"Anyone seen Gallagher?" Bear yelled.

"Took off a few minutes ago. And in one helluva lousy mood. We were glad to get rid of him!"

Bear laughed, or at least his chest rumbled and his huge shoulders shook. "Well, here's the thorn in his side." He nodded at Abby, windblown and pink-cheeked, perched in the seat next to him. "Anyone want to give her a ride downriver?"

"What!" Abby gasped, clenching the door handle. "What? Follow him on the river?"

"If you want to see him anytime soon. Choice is yours."

Abby closed her eyes. Said a quick prayer. Jumped out of the Jeep. "Okay, whose boat do I ride in?"

They were still laughing as the raft pushed off from shore. She heard them although she couldn't see them—not them or anything else, with her eyes squeezed shut and her arms wrapped over her head.

"Hey, this is going to be an easy ride. Enjoy it,"

the oarsman coaxed, but Abby wasn't buying it. She huddled in the bottom of the raft, yelping as it bounced and sped over the water.

Then she felt a hand on her shoulder. "Look up ahead. There he is."

She peeked out, and sure enough, there was Jack, dark head, massive shoulders, broad back. Oh, yes. Jack! "Jack!" she shouted, forgetting everything but him. There he was, right there, almost close enough to grab. "Jack!"

He looked over his shoulder and just about lost his grip on his oars. "What the hell . . . ?" His words were lost in the roar of the river, but she could read his lips, plain as day.

Shaking as she was with fear and hope and desire, she still had to laugh. "Hey, Gallagher! Pull over!" she shouted. "I've got to talk to you!"

He strained at the oars, causing the muscles across his shoulders and back to ripple, reminding her of the very first time she'd seen him, a few months before, a lifetime ago.

And his raft slowed as hers sped to meet him.

"What are you doing here?" he shouted across the water at her.

"I love you," she shouted back.

Her guide shook his head, looking from Abby, crouched in the bottom of his raft, to Jack, dark and fearsome in the other. "Hey, wait a minute, folks! I don't want to get in the middle of this. Gallagher, let me pull a little closer, and she can climb on over to you."

Jack eyed them, and the white water in between, then shook his head. "No way!" he shouted. "She's scared. She'll never do it."

"Want to bet, Gallagher?" Abby snapped. Holding onto the edge of the raft, she crept around to the side nearest Jack. Then she stood up. "Ready for me, Gallagher?" she yelled, and then she held her breath and jumped.

She landed in a tumble against Jack's knees, and grabbed hold of him and held on tightly. "See, Gallagher, I can do anything. I can ride the river, visit Pop and tell him I was sorry I didn't come right away, and talk Bear into bringing me up here. I can do *anything*," she whispered. "I can even change. All it took was the thought that I'd never see you again, that you wouldn't love me the way you do. And that I'd never, ever love anyone else."

Jack hadn't moved, not one muscle; but there was a change in the dark depths of his eyes. Abby looked up and saw herself reflected there.

She drew a shaky little breath and smiled up at him, her pale, heart-shaped face shining. "Oh, Jack, for me other things will always matter; my folks, my sister, even the Paradise—or whatever comes next— but, Jack, you are the center of my life. My heart. *You* are what I could not live without."

He flashed a wild, exultant grin, then aimed the raft at a sandy spot along the bank, dropped the oars, and grabbed her, holding her as if he'd never let go. "Now, that was worth the wait, darlin'!" Then he whispered into her hair, "So you saw Pop? Did he tell you all our plans?"

"What plans?" she echoed, rubbing her cheek against his. "What are you two up to now?"

"Pop decided he'd like to retire. Thinks he'd like to try Florida, so we sold the lodge to that couple from Kansas City for a good price." That old Tom Sawyer grin started at his beautiful mouth and climbed to his dark, shining eyes. "You're going to take half and buy out your new partners, and the Paradise'll be all yours, the way it *should* be. And me, I'm going to open a fishing camp on the St. Johns—or the Withlacoochee—or the Wekiwa—one of those lazy little rivers of yours."

"Oh, Jack, I love you! I love you, love you, love you—and I'll never stop."

"Damn right!"

"Oh, you crazy, wonderful man!"

"Wait—you haven't heard all the conditions. One: I expect a dowry."

"A dowry?" she repeated.

"Yup. I heard you have a fine collection of hand-tied flies."

"They're yours!"

"Oh, you're easy, woman." He kissed the tip of her freckled nose. "Okay. Two: Bear will run the rafting outfit, but I've got to come back at least once a year to ride the rivers. Can you handle that?"

"Handle it? I may even ride them with you, Gallagher, now that I know how to pick the right river rat." She wrapped her arms around his neck and kissed him sweet and hard on the mouth. "The question is, can I handle you?"

"Well, you've got a whole lifetime to find out, darlin'."

THE EDITOR'S CORNER

Next month's LOVESWEPTs are sure to keep you warm as the first crisp winds of autumn nip the air! Rarely do our six books for the month have a common theme, but it just so happens our October group of LOVESWEPTs all deal with characters who must come to terms with their pasts in order to learn to love from the heart again.

In **RENEGADE,** LOVESWEPT #282, Judy Gill reunites a pair of lovers who have so many reasons for staying together, but who are pulled apart by old hurts. (Both have emotional scars that haven't yet healed.) When Jacqueline Train and Renny Knight struck a deal two years earlier, neither one expected their love to flourish in a marriage that had been purely a practical arrangement. And when Renny returns to claim her, Jacqueline is filled with panic . . . and sudden hope. But with tenderness, compassion, and overwhelming love Renny teaches her that the magic they'd created before was only a prelude to their real and enduring happiness.

LOVESWEPT #283, **ON WINGS OF FLAME,** is Gail Douglas's first published romance and one that is sure to establish her as a winner in the genre. When Jed Brannen offers Kelly Flynn the job of immortalizing his uncle's beloved pet in stained glass, she knows it's just a ploy on Jed's part. He's desperate to rekindle the romance that he'd walked away from years before. He'd been her Indiana Jones, roaming the globe in search of danger, and she'd almost managed to banish the memory of his tender caresses—until he returns in search of the only woman he's ever loved. Kelly's wounded pride makes her hold back from forgiving him, but every time she runs from him, she stumbles and falls . . . right into his arms.

Fayrene Preston brings you a jewel of a book in **EMERALD SUNSHINE,** LOVESWEPT #284. Too dazzled by the bright blue Dallas sky to keep her mind on the road, heroine Kathy Broderick rides her bike smack into Paul Garth's sleek limousine! The condition of her mangled bike isn't nearly as important to Kathy, however, as the condition of her heart when Paul offers her his help—

(continued)

and then his love. But resisting this man and the passionate hunger she feels for him, she finds, is as futile as pedaling backward. Paul has a few dark secrets he doesn't know how to share with Kathy. But as in all her romances, Fayrene brings these two troubled people together in a joyous union that won't fail to touch your soul.

TUCKER BOONE, LOVESWEPT #285, is Joan Elliott Pickart at her best! Alison Murdock has her work cut out for her as a lawyer who finds delivering Tucker's inheritance—an English butler—no small task. Swearing he's no gentleman, Tucker decides to uncover Alison's playful side—a side of herself she'd buried long ago under ambition and determination. Alison almost doesn't stop to consider what rugged, handsome Tucker Boone is doing to her orderly life, until talk of the future makes her remember the past—and her vow to rise to the top of her profession. Luckily Tucker convinces her that reaching new heights in his arms is the most important goal of all!

Kay Hooper has written the romance you've all been waiting for! In **SHADES OF GRAY,** LOVESWEPT #286, Kay tells the love story of the charismatic island ruler, Andres Sereno, first introduced in **RAFFERTY'S WIFE** last November. Sara Marsh finds that loving the man who'd abducted her to keep her safe from his enemies is something as elemental to her as breathing. But when Sara sees the violent side of Andres, she can't reconcile it with the sensitive, exquisitely passionate man she knows him to be. Andres realizes that loving Sara fuels the goodness in him, fills him with urgent need. And Sara can't control the force of her love for Andres any more than he can stop himself from doing what must be done to save his island of Kadeira. Suddenly she learns that nothing appears black and white to her anymore. She can see only shades of gray . . . and all the hues of love.

Following her debut as a LOVESWEPT author with her book **DIVINE DESIGN,** published in June, Mary Kay McComas is back on the scene with her second book for us, **OBSESSION,** LOVESWEPT #287. A powerful tale of a woman overcoming the injustices of her past with the help of a man who knows her more intimately than

(continued)

any other person on earth—before he even meets her—Mary Kay weaves an emotional web of romance and desire. Esther Brite is known to the world as a famous songwriter, one half of a the husband and wife team that brought music into the lives of millions. But when her husband and son are killed in a car accident, Esther returns to her hometown, where she'd once been shunned, searching for answers to questions she isn't sure she wants to ask. Doctor Dan Jacobey has reasons of his own for seeking sanctuary in the town of Bellewood—the one place where he could feel close to the woman he'd become obsessed with—Esther Brite. Esther and Dan discover that together they are not afraid to face the demons of the past and promise each other a beautiful tomorrow.

I think you're going to savor and enjoy each of the books next month as if you were feasting on a gourmet six-course meal!

Bon appetite!

Carolyn Nichols

Carolyn Nichols
  Editor
LOVESWEPT
Bantam Books
666 Fifth Avenue
New York, NY 10103

ON SALE THIS MONTH
A novel you won't want to miss

SO MANY PROMISES
By Nomi Berger

The moving story of Kirsten Harald's triumph
over her shattered past . . . her victory in
finding and holding the one great love of her life.

THE HOMETOWN HUNK CONTEST

FOR EVERY WOMAN WHO HAS EVER SAID—
"I know a man who looks
just like the hero of this book"
—HAVE WE GOT A CONTEST FOR YOU!

To help celebrate our fifth year of publishing LOVESWEPT we are having a fabulous, fun-filled event called THE HOMETOWN HUNK contest. We are going to reissue six classic early titles by six of your favorite authors.

> **DARLING OBSTACLES by Barbara Boswell**
> **IN A CLASS BY ITSELF by Sandra Brown**
> **C.J.'S FATE by Kay Hooper**
> **THE LADY AND THE UNICORN by Iris Johansen**
> **CHARADE by Joan Elliott Pickart**
> **FOR THE LOVE OF SAMI by Fayrene Preston**

Here, as in the backs of all July, August, and September 1988 LOVESWEPTS you will find "cover notes" just like the ones we prepare at Bantam as the background for our art director to create our covers. These notes will describe the hero and heroine, give a teaser on the plot, and suggest a scene for the cover. Your part in the contest will be to see if a great looking local man—or men, if your hometown is so blessed—fits our description of one of the heroes of the six books we will reissue.

THE HOMETOWN HUNK who is selected (one for each of the six titles) will be flown to New York via United Airlines and will stay at the Loews Summit Hotel—the ideal hotel for business or pleasure in midtown Manhattan—for two nights. All travel arrangements made by Reliable Travel International, Incorporated. He will be the model for the new cover of the book which will be released in mid-1989. The six people who send in the winning photos of their HOMETOWN HUNK will receive a pre-selected assortment of LOVESWEPT books free for one year. Please see the Official Rules above the Official Entry Form for full details and restrictions.

We can't wait to start judging those pictures! Oh, and you must let the man you've chosen know that you're entering him in the contest. After all, if he wins he'll have to come to New York.

Have fun. Here's your chance to get the cover-lover of your dreams!

Carolyn Nichols

Carolyn Nichols
Editor
LOVESWEPT
Bantam Books
666 Fifth Avenue
New York, NY 10102—0023

THE HOMETOWN HUNK CONTEST

DARLING OBSTACLES
(Originally Published as LOVESWEPT #95)
By Barbara Boswell

COVER NOTES

The Characters:

Hero:
GREG WILDER's gorgeous body and "to-die-for" good looks haven't hurt him in the dating department, but when most women discover he's a widower with four kids, they head for the hills! Greg has the hard, muscular build of an athlete, and his light brown hair, which he wears neatly parted on the side, is streaked blond by the sun. Add to that his aquamarine blue eyes that sparkle when he laughs, and his sensual mouth and generous lower lip, and you're probably wondering what woman in her right mind wouldn't want Greg's strong, capable surgeon's hands working their magic on her—kids or no kids!

Personality Traits:
An acclaimed neurosurgeon, Greg Wilder is a celebrity of sorts in the planned community of Woodland, Maryland. Authoritative, debonair, self-confident, his reputation for engaging in one casual relationship after another almost overshadows his prowess as a doctor. In reality, Greg dates more out of necessity than anything else, since he has to attend one social function after another. He considers most of the events boring and wishes he could spend more time with his children. But his profession is a difficult and demanding one—and being both father and mother to four kids isn't any less so. A thoughtful, generous, sometimes befuddled father, Greg tries to do it all. Cerebral, he uses his intellect and skill rather than physical strength to win his victories. However, he never expected to come up against one Mary Magdalene May!

Heroine:
MARY MAGDALENE MAY, called Maggie by her friends, is the thirty-two-year-old mother of three children. She has shoulder-length auburn hair, and green eyes that shout her Irish heritage. With high cheekbones and an upturned nose covered with a smattering of freckles, Maggie thinks of herself more as the girl-next-door type. Certainly, she believes, she could never be one of Greg Wilder's beautiful escorts.

Setting: The small town of Woodland, Maryland

The Story:
Surgeon Greg Wilder wanted to court the feisty and beautiful widow who'd been caring for his four kids, but she just wouldn't let him past her doorstep! Sure that his interest was only casual, and that he preferred more sophisticated women, Maggie May vowed to keep Greg at arm's length. But he wouldn't take no for an answer. And once he'd crashed through her defenses and pulled her into his arms, he was tireless—and reckless—in his campaign to win her over. Maggie had found it tough enough to resist one determined doctor; now he threatened to call in his kids and hers as reinforcements—seven rowdy snags to romance!

Cover scene:
As if romancing Maggie weren't hard enough, Greg can't seem to find time to spend with her without their children around. Stealing a private moment on the stairs in Maggie's house, Greg and Maggie embrace. She is standing one step above him, but she still has to look up at him to see into his eyes. Greg's hands are on her hips, and her hands are resting on his shoulders. Maggie is wearing a very sheer, short pink nightgown, and Greg has on wheat-colored jeans and a navy and yellow striped rugby shirt. Do they have time to kiss?

THE HOMETOWN HUNK CONTEST

IN A CLASS BY ITSELF
(Originally Published as LOVESWEPT #66)
By Sandra Brown

COVER NOTES

The Characters:

Hero:

LOGAN WEBSTER would have no trouble posing for a Scandinavian travel poster. His wheat-colored hair always seems to be tousled, defying attempts to control it, and falls across his wide forehead. Thick eyebrows one shade darker than his hair accentuate his crystal blue eyes. He has a slender nose that flairs slightly over a mouth that testifies to both sensitivity and strength. The faint lines around his eyes and alongside his mouth give the impression that reaching the ripe age of 30 wasn't all fun and games for him. Logan's square, determined jaw is punctuated by a vertical cleft. His broad shoulders and narrow waist add to his tall, lean appearance.

Personality traits:

Logan Webster has had to scrape and save and fight for everything he's gotten. Born into a poor farm family, he was driven to succeed and overcome his "wrong side of the tracks" image. His businesses include cattle, real estate, and natural gas. Now a pillar of the community, Logan's life has been a true rags-to-riches story. Only Sandra Brown's own words can describe why he is masculinity epitomized: "Logan had 'the walk,' that saddle-tramp saunter that was inherent to native Texan men, passed down through generations of cowboys. It was, without even trying to be, sexy. The unconscious roll of the hips, the slow strut, the flexed knees, the slouching stance, the deceptive laziness that hid a latent aggressiveness." Wow! And not only does he have "the walk," but he's fun and generous and kind. Even with his wealth, he feels at home living in his small hometown with simple, hard-working, middle-class, backbone-of-America folks. A born leader, people automatically gravitate toward him.

Heroine:
DANI QUINN is a sophisticated twenty-eight-year-old woman. Dainty, her body compact, she is utterly feminine. Dani's pale, lustrous hair is moonlight and honey spun together, and because it is very straight, she usually wears it in a chignon. With golden eyes to match her golden hair, Dani is the one woman Logan hasn't been able to get off his mind for the ten years they've been apart.

Setting: Primarily on Logan's ranch in East Texas.

The Story:
Ten years had passed since Dani Quinn had graduated from high school in the small Texas town, ten years since the night her elopement with Logan Webster had ended in disaster. Now Dani approached her tenth reunion with uncertainty. Logan would be there . . . Logan, the only man who'd ever made her shiver with desire and need, but would she have the courage to face the fury in his eyes? She couldn't defend herself against his anger and hurt—to do so would demand she reveal the secret sorrow she shared with no one. Logan's touch had made her his so long ago. Could he reach past the pain to make her his for all time?

Cover Scene:
It's sunset, and Logan and Dani are standing beside the swimming pool on his ranch, embracing. The pool is surrounded by semitropical plants and lush flower beds. In the distance, acres of rolling pasture land resembling a green lake undulate into dense, piney woods. Dani is wearing a strapless, peacock blue bikini and sandals with leather ties that wrap around her ankles. Her hair is straight and loose, falling to the middle of her back. Logan has on a light-colored pair of corduroy shorts and a short-sleeved designer knit shirt in a pale shade of yellow.

THE HOMETOWN HUNK CONTEST

C.J.'S FATE
(Originally Published as LOVESWEPT #32)
By Kay Hooper

COVER NOTES

The Characters:

Hero:
FATE WESTON easily could have walked straight off an Indian reservation. His raven black hair and strong, well-molded features testify to his heritage. But somewhere along the line genetics threw Fate a curve—his eyes are the deepest, darkest blue imaginable! Above those blue eyes are dark slanted eyebrows, and fanning out from those eyes are faint laugh lines—the only sign of the fact that he's thirty-four years old. Tall, Fate moves with easy, loose-limbed grace. Although he isn't an athlete, Fate takes very good care of himself, and it shows in his strong physique. Striking at first glance and fascinating with each succeeding glance, the serious expressions on his face make him look older than his years, but with one smile he looks boyish again.

Personality traits:
Fate possesses a keen sense of humor. His heavy-lidded, intelligent eyes are capable of concealment, but there is a shrewdness in them that reveals the man hadn't needed college or a law degree to be considered intelligent. The set of his head tells you that he is proud—perhaps even a bit arrogant. He is attractive and perfectly well aware of that fact. Unconventional, paradoxical, tender, silly, lusty, gentle, comical, serious, absurd, and endearing are all words that come to mind when you think of Fate. He is not ashamed to be everything a man can be. A defense attorney by profession, one can detect a bit of frustrated actor in his character. More than anything else, though, it's the

impression of humor about him—reinforced by the elusive dimple in his cheek—that makes Fate Weston a scrumptious hero!

Heroine:
C.J. ADAMS is a twenty-six-year-old research librarian. Unaware of her own attractiveness, C.J. tends to play down her pixylike figure and tawny gold eyes. But once she meets Fate, she no longer feels that her short, burnished copper curls and the sprinkling of freckles on her nose make her unappealing. He brings out the vixen in her, and changes the smart, bookish woman who professed to have no interest in men into the beautiful, sexy woman she really was all along. Now, if only he could get her to tell him what C.J. stands for!

Setting: Ski lodge in Aspen, Colorado

The Story:
C.J. Adams had been teased enough about her seeming lack of interest in the opposite sex. On a ski trip with her five best friends, she impulsively embraced a handsome stranger, pretending they were secret lovers—and the delighted lawyer who joined in her impetuous charade seized the moment to deepen the kiss. Astonished at his reaction, C.J. tried to nip their romance in the bud—but found herself nipping at his neck instead! She had met her match in a man who could answer her witty remarks with clever ripostes of his own, and a lover whose caresses aroused in her a passionate need she'd never suspected that she could feel. Had destiny somehow tossed them together?

Cover Scene:
C.J. and Fate virtually have the ski slopes to themselves early one morning, and they take advantage of it! Frolicking in a snow drift, Fate is covering C.J. with snow—and kisses! They are flushed from the cold weather and from the excitement of being in love. C.J. is wearing a sky-blue, one-piece, tight-fitting ski outfit that zips down the front. Fate is wearing a navy blue parka and matching ski pants.

THE HOMETOWN HUNK CONTEST

THE LADY AND THE UNICORN
(Originally Published as LOVESWEPT #29)
By Iris Johansen

COVER NOTES

The Characters:

Hero:
Not classically handsome. RAFE SANTINE's blunt, craggy
features reinforce the quality of overpowering virility about
him. He has wide, Slavic cheekbones and a bold, thrust-
ing chin, which give the impression of strength and authority. Thick black eyebrows are set over piercing dark
eyes. He wears his heavy, dark hair long. His large frame
measures in at almost six feet four inches, and it's hard to
believe that a man with such brawny shoulders and strong
thighs could exhibit the pantherlike grace which charac-
terizes Rafe's movements. Rafe Santine is definitely a man
to be reckoned with, and heroine Janna Cannon does just
that!

Personality traits:
Our hero is a man who radiates an aura of power and
danger, and women find him intriguing and irresistible.
Rafe Santine is a self-made billionaire at the age of thirty-
eight. Almost entirely self-educated, he left school at sixteen to work on his first construction job, and by the time
he was twenty-three, he owned the company. From there
he branched out into real estate, computers, and oil. Rafe
reportedly changes mistresses as often as he changes shirts.
His reputation for ruthless brilliance has been earned over
years of fighting to the top of the economic ladder from
the slums of New York. His gruff manner and hard personality hide the tender, vulnerable side of him. Rafe also
possesses an insatiable thirst for knowledge that is a
passion with him. Oddly enough, he has a wry sense of

humor that surfaces unexpectedly from time to time. And, though cynical to the extreme, he never lets his natural skepticism interfere with his innate sense of justice.

Heroine:
JANNA CANNON, a game warden for a small wildlife preserve, is a very dedicated lady. She is tall at five feet nine inches and carries herself in a stately way. Her long hair is dark brown and is usually twisted into a single thick braid in back. Of course, Rafe never lets her keep her hair braided when they make love! Janna is one quarter Cherokee Indian by heritage, and she possesses the dark eyes and skin of her ancestors.

Setting: Rafe's estate in Carmel, California

The Story:
Janna Cannon scaled the high walls of Rafe Santine's private estate, afraid of nothing and determined to appeal to the powerful man who could save her beloved animal preserve. She bewitched his guard dogs, then cast a spell of enchantment over him as well. Janna's profound grace, her caring nature, made the tough and proud Rafe grow mercurial in her presence. She offered him a gift he'd never risked reaching out for before—but could he trust his own emotions enough to open himself to her love?

Cover Scene:
In the gazebo overlooking the rugged cliffs at the edge of the Pacific Ocean, Rafe and Janna share a passionate moment together. The gazebo is made of redwood and the interior is small and cozy. Scarlet cushions cover the benches, and matching scarlet curtains hang from the eaves, caught back by tasseled sashes to permit the sea breeze to whip through the enclosure. Rafe is wearing black suede pants and a charcoal gray crew-neck sweater. Janna is wearing a safari-style khaki shirt-and-slacks outfit and suede desert boots. They embrace against the breathtaking backdrop of wild, crashing, white-crested waves pounding the rocks and cliffs below.

THE HOMETOWN HUNK CONTEST

CHARADE
(Originally Published as LOVESWEPT #74)
By Joan Elliott Pickart

COVER NOTES

The Characters:

Hero:
The phrase tall, dark, and handsome was coined to describe TENNES WHITNEY. His coal black hair reaches past his collar in back, and his fathomless steel gray eyes are framed by the kind of thick, dark lashes that a woman would kill to have. Darkly tanned, Tennes has a straight nose and a square chin, with—you guessed it!—a Kirk Douglas cleft. Tennes oozes masculinity and virility. He's a handsome son-of-a-gun!

Personality traits:
A shrewd, ruthless business tycoon, Tennes is a man of strength and principle. He's perfected the art of buying floundering companies and turning them around financially, then selling them at a profit. He possesses a sixth sense about business—in short, he's a winner! But there are two sides to his personality. Always in cool command, Tennes, who fears no man or challenge, is rendered emotionally vulnerable when faced with his elderly aunt's illness. His deep devotion to the woman who raised him clearly casts him as a warm, compassionate guy—not at all like the tough-as-nails executive image he presents. Leave it to heroine Whitney Jordan to discover the real man behind the complicated enigma.

Heroine:
WHITNEY JORDAN's russet-colored hair floats past her shoulders in glorious waves. Her emerald green eyes, full breasts, and long, slender legs—not to mention her peaches-

and-cream complexion—make her eye-poppingly attractive. How can Tennes resist the twenty-six-year-old beauty? And how can Whitney consider becoming serious with him? If their romance flourishes, she may end up being Whitney Whitney!

Setting: Los Angeles, California

The Story:
One moment writer Whitney Jordan was strolling the aisles of McNeil's Department Store, plotting the untimely demise of a soap opera heartthrob; the next, she was nearly knocked over by a real-life stunner who implored her to be his fiancée! The ailing little gray-haired aunt who'd raised him had one final wish, he said—to see her dear nephew Tennes married to the wonderful girl he'd described in his letters . . . only that girl hadn't existed—until now! Tennes promised the masquerade would last only through lunch, but Whitney gave such an inspired performance that Aunt Olive refused to let her go. And what began as a playful romantic deception grew more breathlessly real by the minute. . . .

Cover Scene:
Whitney's living room is bright and cheerful. The gray carpeting and blue sofa with green and blue throw pillows gives the apartment a cool but welcoming appearance. Sitting on the sofa next to Tennes, Whitney is wearing a black crepe dress that is simply cut but stunning. It is cut low over her breasts and held at the shoulders by thin straps. The skirt falls to her knees in soft folds and the bodice is nipped in at the waist with a matching belt. She has on black high heels, but prefers not to wear any jewelry to spoil the simplicity of the dress. Tennes is dressed in a black suit with a white silk shirt and a deep red tie.

THE HOMETOWN HUNK CONTEST

FOR THE LOVE OF SAMI
(Originally Published as LOVESWEPT #34)
By Fayrene Preston

COVER NOTES

Hero:
DANIEL PARKER-ST. JAMES is every woman's dream come true. With glossy black hair and warm, reassuring blue eyes, he makes our heroine melt with just a glance. Daniel's lean face is chiseled into assertive planes. His lips are full and firmly sculptured, and his chin has the determined and arrogant thrust to it only a man who's sure of himself can carry off. Daniel has a lot in common with Clark Kent. Both wear glasses, and when Daniel removes them to make love to Sami, she thinks he really is Superman!

Personality traits:
Daniel Parker-St. James is one of the Twin Cities' most respected attorneys. He's always in the news, either in the society columns with his latest society lady, or on the front page with his headline cases. He's brilliant and takes on only the toughest cases—usually those that involve millions of dollars. Daniel has a reputation for being a deadly opponent in the courtroom. Because he's from a socially prominent family and is a Harvard graduate, it's expected that he'll run for the Senate one day. Distinguished-looking and always distinctively dressed—he's fastidious about his appearance—Daniel gives off an unassailable air of authority and absolute control.

Heroine:
SAMUELINA (SAMI) ADKINSON is secretly a wealthy heiress. No one would guess. She lives in a converted warehouse loft, dresses to suit no one but herself, and dabbles in the creative arts. Sami is twenty-six years old, with

long, honey-colored hair. She wears soft, wispy bangs and has very thick brown lashes framing her golden eyes. Of medium height, Sami has to look up to gaze into Daniel's deep blue eyes.

Setting: St. Paul, Minnesota

The Story:
Unpredictable heiress Sami Adkinson had endeared herself to the most surprising people—from the bag ladies in the park she protected . . . to the mobster who appointed himself her guardian . . . to her exasperated but loving friends. Then Sami was arrested while demonstrating to save baby seals, and it took powerful attorney Daniel Parker-St. James to bail her out. Daniel was smitten, soon cherishing Sami and protecting her from her night fears. Sami reveled in his love—and resisted it too. And holding on to Sami, Daniel discovered, was like trying to hug quicksilver. . . .

Cover Scene:
The interior of Daniel's house is very grand and supremely formal, the decor sophisticated, refined, and quietly tasteful, just like Daniel himself. Rich traditional fabrics cover plush oversized custom sofas and Regency wing chairs. Queen Anne furniture is mixed with Chippendale and is subtly complemented with Oriental accent pieces. In the library, floor-to-ceiling bookcases filled with rare books provide the backdrop for Sami and Daniel's embrace. Sami is wearing a gold satin sheath gown. The dress has a high neckline, but in back is cut provocatively to the waist. Her jewels are exquisite. The necklace is made up of clusters of flowers created by large, flawless diamonds. From every cluster a huge, perfectly matched teardrop emerald hangs. The earrings are composed of an even larger flower cluster, and an equally huge teardrop-shaped emerald hangs from each one. Daniel is wearing a classic, elegant tuxedo.

LOVESWEPT® HOMETOWN HUNK CONTEST

OFFICIAL RULES

> IN A CLASS BY ITSELF by Sandra Brown
> FOR THE LOVE OF SAMI by Fayrene Preston
> C.J.'S FATE by Kay Hooper
> THE LADY AND THE UNICORN by Iris Johansen
> CHARADE by Joan Elliott Pickart
> DARLING OBSTACLES by Barbara Boswell

1. NO PURCHASE NECESSARY. Enter the HOMETOWN HUNK contest by completing the Official Entry Form below and enclosing a sharp color full-length photograph (easy to see details, with the photo being no smaller than 2½″ × 3½″) of the man you think perfectly represents one of the heroes from the above-listed books which are described in the accompanying Loveswept cover notes. Please be sure to fill out the Official Entry Form completely, and also be sure to clearly print on the back of the man's photograph the man's name, address, city, state, zip code, telephone number, date of birth, your name, address, city, state, zip code, telephone number, your relationship, if any, to the man (e.g. wife, girlfriend) as well as the title of the Loveswept book for which you are entering the man. If you do not have an Official Entry Form, you can print all of the required information on a 3″ × 5″ card and attach it to the photograph with all the necessary information printed on the back of the photograph as well. YOUR HERO MUST SIGN BOTH THE BACK OF THE OFFICIAL ENTRY FORM (OR 3″ × 5″ CARD) AND THE PHOTOGRAPH TO SIGNIFY HIS CONSENT TO BEING ENTERED IN THE CONTEST. Completed entries should be sent to:

> BANTAM BOOKS
> HOMETOWN HUNK CONTEST
> Department CN
> 666 Fifth Avenue
> New York, New York 10102–0023

All photographs and entries become the property of Bantam Books and will not be returned under any circumstances.

2. Six men will be chosen by the Loveswept authors as a HOMETOWN HUNK (one HUNK per Loveswept title). By entering the contest, each winner and each person who enters a winner agrees to abide by Bantam Books' rules and to be subject to Bantam Books' eligibility requirements. Each winning HUNK and each person who enters a winner will be required to sign all papers deemed necessary by Bantam Books before receiving any prize. Each winning HUNK will be flown via **United Airlines** from his closest United Airlines-serviced city to New York City and will stay at the **Suss tt** Hotel—the ideal hotel for business or pleasure in midtown Manhattan—for two nights. Winning HUNKS' meals and hotel transfers will be provided by Bantam Books. Travel and hotel arrangements are made by **RELIABLE TRAVEL INTERNATIONAL INC** and are subject to availability and to Bantam Books' date requirements. Each winning HUNK will pose with a female model at a photographer's studio for a photograph that will serve as the basis of a Loveswept front cover. Each winning HUNK will receive a $150.00 modeling fee. Each winning HUNK will be required to sign an Affidavit of Eligibility and Model's Release supplied by Bantam Books. (Approximate retail value of HOMETOWN HUNK'S PRIZE: $900.00). The six people who send in a winning HOMETOWN HUNK photograph that is used by Bantam will receive free for one year each, LOVESWEPT romance paperback books published by Bantam during that year. (Approximate retail value: $180.00.) Each person who submits a winning photograph

will also be required to sign an Affidavit of Eligibility and Promotional Release supplied by Bantam Books. All winning HUNKS' (as well as the people who submit the winning photographs) names, addresses, biographical data and likenesses may be used by Bantam Books for publicity and promotional purposes without any additional compensation. There will be no prize substitutions or cash equivalents made.

3. All completed entries must be received by Bantam Books no later than September 15, 1988. Bantam Books is not responsible for lost or misdirected entries. The finalists will be selected by Loveswept editors and the six winning HOMETOWN HUNKS will be selected by the six authors of the participating Loveswept books. Winners will be selected on the basis of how closely the judges believe they reflect the descriptions of the books' heroes. Winners will be notified on or about October 31, 1988. If there are insufficient entries or if in the judges' opinions, no entry is suitable or adequately reflects the descriptions of the hero(s) in the book(s), Bantam may decide not to award a prize for the applicable book(s) and may reissue the book(s) at its discretion.

4. The contest is open to residents of the U.S. and Canada, except the Province of Quebec, and is void where prohibited by law. All federal and local regulations apply. Employees of Reliable Travel International, Inc., United Airlines, the Summit Hotel, and the Bantam Doubleday Dell Publishing Group, Inc., their subsidiaries and affiliates, and their immediate families are ineligible to enter.

5. For an extra copy of the Official Rules, the Official Entry Form, and the accompanying Loveswept cover notes, send your request and a self-addressed stamped envelope (Vermont and Washington State residents need not affix postage) before August 20, 1988 to the address listed in Paragraph 1 above.

LOVESWEPT'S HOMETOWN HUNK OFFICIAL ENTRY FORM

BANTAM BOOKS
HOMETOWN HUNK CONTEST
Dept. CN
666 Fifth Avenue
New York, New York 10102–0023

HOMETOWN HUNK CONTEST

YOUR NAME_____

YOUR ADDRESS_____

CITY_____ STATE_____ ZIP_____

THE NAME OF THE LOVESWEPT BOOK FOR WHICH YOU ARE ENTERING THIS PHOTO

_____by_____

YOUR RELATIONSHIP TO YOUR HERO_____

YOUR HERO'S NAME_____

YOUR HERO'S ADDRESS_____

CITY_____ STATE_____ ZIP_____

YOUR HERO'S TELEPHONE #_____

YOUR HERO'S DATE OF BIRTH_____

YOUR HERO'S SIGNATURE CONSENTING TO HIS PHOTOGRAPH ENTRY

_____